P9-DGR-328

MAGGIE TWOHILL

SUPERBOWL

UPSET

Bradbury Press/New York

Collier Macmillan Canada/Toronto
Maxwell Macmillan International Publishing Group
New York/Oxford/Singapore/Sydney

This is for Robyn Brady
and her super family

Bradbury Press
Macmillan Publishing Company
866 Third Avenue
New York, NY 10022

Collier Macmillan Canada, Inc.
1200 Eglinton Avenue East
Suite 200
Don Mills, Ontario M3C 3N1

First edition
Printed in the United States of America
1 2 3 4 5 6 7 8 9 10

The text of this book is set in Aster.
Book design by Cathy Bobak

Library of Congress Cataloging-in-Publication Data
Twohill, Maggie.
Superbowl upset / by Maggie Twohill. -- 1st ed.
p.   cm.
Summary: Two bickering stepchildren find little time to argue with
each other when they join Mom and Dad on a calamity-filled trip to
the Superbowl.
ISBN 0-02-789691-9
[1. Stepchildren--Fiction.   2. Super Bowl Game (Football)--
Fiction.]   I. Title.
PZ7.T93Su   1991
[Fic]--dc20   90-47412

ALSO BY MAGGIE TWOHILL

Bigmouth
Jeeter, Mason and the Magic Headset
Who Has the Lucky-Duck in Class 4-B?

CONTENTS

ONE

KICKOFF

Lucas bit off the end of a roll and glanced over at his stepsister. Ginger looked up at her stepbrother and then quickly back down at her plate. He's planning something mean, she thought. He's too quiet.

Their parents smiled at each other as they nibbled on their end-of-Christmas-vacation meal—the last of the turkey hash.

Beaming down at all of them from the shelf over the sideboard were silver-framed photographs of their new family: Lucas's mother, Marcia, in her baby blue chiffon wedding dress, looking up at Ginger's father, Arthur, whose fingers seemed to be mashing the corsage on Marcia's wrist; next to them stood Marcia's brother Marvin and his wife, the best man and matron of honor; Ginger and Lucas were in front, dressed in their Sunday best and trying hard to smile at each other for their parents' sakes. There were favorite pictures from before the wedding, too: Uncle Marvin and Aunt Sudie, pointing over a stone wall in wonderment at Niagara Falls; Lucas, grinning happily, cheek to cheek with his dog, Frank; Ginger, her arms raised in a victory sign after scoring a goal for her Kids' League hockey team.

She scored that goal off *me,* Lucas thought, scraping his fork against his plate.

"Careful, dear," Marcia murmured, her mouth full of turkey.

Wagging his tail, Frank turned around under the table, hoping for a scrap to be sneaked his way.

Ginger sighed and poked at her peas. She was almost glad Christmas vacation was at an end. She was *definitely* glad the turkey hash was, too.

Lucas rolled his eyes up again to the photo of Ginger's hockey goal, then quickly reached across the table and tipped her glass so that milk dribbled over her gravy, vegetables, and mashed turkey.

Lucas put his hands in his lap and bent over his own plate.

"Aaaaahhhhhgggg!" Ginger screamed. *"Look what Lucas did!"*

"What? Who? Me?" Lucas looked up, wide-eyed.

"He poured milk in my dinner!"

"I did not. I'm just sitting here, minding my own business."

"He did too!"

"Did not."

"Did too!"

"Did not."

"Stop!" Lucas's mother inhaled loudly through her nose the way she always did when she was about to get mad.

"That's enough from both of you!" Ginger's father glowered across the table at them.

Under the table Frank growled. Then there was silence again in the room.

Lucas's mother raised her eyebrows at Ginger's father, and they both heaved an enormous sigh at each other.

It had been like this for four months—ever since the wedding. Lucas's mother had been divorced since Lucas was a baby, so Lucas was happy when she met a nice man. Ginger's father had been widowed since Ginger was a baby, so she was glad when he came home after a party saying he'd met "her." Arthur and Marcia were thrilled to have found each other and fallen in love.

But then, Ginger and Lucas found out just whose parents were whose, and the excitement wore off quickly.

"Oh, Mom, not Gin-ger Bid-well's father!" Lucas groaned.

"Daddy! Lu-cas Rid-ley's *mother?*" Ginger wailed.

Lucas and Ginger had known each other for years. Not only were they in the same grade—fifth—but they were in the same class. They competed in sports—Kids' League Hockey—they argued over schoolwork, and they didn't like each other's friends.

However:

Ginger liked Lucas's mom very much. She was kind. She listened to Ginger with a woman's ear, and it was a lovely change to have a mother as well as a father. And even though Marcia worked full-time for a women's newsletter and did most of the writing and publishing herself, she still found time to help Ginger with her homework and to bake

5

gingerbread men for the entire fifth grade's Christmas party.

Lucas liked Ginger's dad very much. It was great having a man's point of view, especially a man like Arthur who seemed to understand Lucas very well. And even though he took the train every day to the city, where he worked hard in an advertising office, he still found time to help Lucas with his homework, play computer games, and take both Lucas and Ginger to baseball, basketball, football, and hockey games.

The three were avid sports fans. Lucas's mother wasn't.

The part that gave Ginger and Lucas a hard time was the part that had to do with being sister and brother.

"I want your mother to be my mom!" Ginger had yelled. "I just want *you* to go live somewhere else!"

To which Lucas had replied, "Stuff it in your ear!"

When their parents had begun to see

each other, Ginger's friends teased her unmercifully.

"Eee-yew, Lucas might change his name to *yours*!" Cindy, Ginger's best friend, had shrieked. "You'll be Ginger and Lucas BID-well! Eee-yew!"

"He better *not* change his name," Ginger had answered. "It's *my* name and my dad's. Not his!"

"Ha, ha, you'll have to live in the same house with Lucas Rid-ley, and he probably has white mice he'll put in your bed!" Ellie had cried. "Maybe you'll have to share a room, even!"

"I will not have to share a room!" Ginger yelled. "And he doesn't have mice, only a yappy dog!"

But their parents had married anyway. Ginger still called herself Ginger Bidwell and her father still called himself Arthur Bidwell. But Lucas's mother now called herself Marcia Ridley-Bidwell, while Lucas stuck to plain old Lucas Ridley.

It was confusing.

Ginger hated to sort the mail.

"It's not a big deal," Lucas had said. "It's just like camp. Everyone's name is different, but you all live in the same tent."

"It's not like camp," Ginger muttered.

Dinners were usually the worst. They were supposed to be the quiet, "together" time. The catching-up-on-our-day time. The family time.

Instead, they were mostly like this one, tonight—Lucas dumping milk onto Ginger's plate, or Ginger kicking at Lucas's foot, with Frank yapping under the table.

The meal had started hopefully at first (as it usually did). Marcia and Arthur had smiled at Ginger's red head and Lucas's brown one as the children bent over their plates, and then they smiled at each other. But as it all slid downhill (as it usually did), each of them had the same thought: This vacation has gone on too long.

"Lucas, you finish eating and go to your room," his mother said.

"But I want to watch TV!"

"Too bad, young man, you should have thought of that before!"

"Ginger, you get yourself another plate in the kitchen and then you go to your room," her father said.

"But I didn't *do* anything!" Ginger wailed.

"The two of you better learn to get along!" Arthur said firmly. His voice was raised. He was feeling the effects of a long day.

Frank began to yap and tug at the cuffs of Arthur's trousers. That made Lucas laugh. It made Ginger laugh, too, because now she was angry at her father for sending her to her room. (Even though she was happy to go to her room.)

"Go get your dinner, now!" Arthur bellowed, shaking Frank off his trousers.

"I'll get it for her," Lucas said, and jumped up from the table.

Marcia and Ginger gaped at him.

He came back to the table with a new plate of hash and set it down in front of Ginger.

"Thanks!" she said, bewildered.

"Oh, that's okay," Lucas answered cheerfully.

"Lucas?"

"What, Mom?"

"You still have to go to your room after dinner."

TWO

THE PLAYERS

Wasn't fair.

Ginger was a big pain.

Lucas flopped back on his bed with his hands on the pillow behind his head.

He looked around.

Okay. It was a nice room. Arthur had done an okay job fixing it up for him. Actually, it was very nice ... but it wasn't his. Not really. Not yet.

The Ridleys had moved into the Bidwell house, which made Ginger happy but bugged Lucas.

"Why can't we stay in *this* house?" he'd wailed, to which his mother answered, "Because Arthur's house is bigger and he has three bedrooms instead of two so that you and Ginger can have your own rooms."

Very sensible.

But it meant that Lucas had had to say good-bye to the "height markings" on his closet door that his mother had started when he was two and had continued until now. He'd had to say good-bye to his favorite nooks and crannies and the view of the Tudor Lake High School football field from his bedroom window. He'd had to say good-bye to home.

Ginger had had to say good-bye to privacy. The shared bathroom was a drag, but worst of all was the noise. She and her dad were pretty quiet people, but the Ridleys seemed to thrive on lots of *sound.* The stereo played along with the television and Lucas and his mom liked to yell over that.

Even their dog liked noise.

Frank. He was small and curly haired and cute, friendly to everyone but Arthur, whose trouser legs he treated like a Christmas bone. Frank yapped loudly whenever anyone stepped into the house, whether they'd been at work or school all day or just down the street for a newspaper or a soda.

The Bidwell-Ridley household was hectic.

"We knew it would be tough at first," Marcia had said to Arthur.

"Right. If we just manage to survive awhile, it'll seem to the kids we've all lived together forever," Arthur had replied.

"You think so?"

"Sure I do."

"Really?"

"Really."

"Eee-yew, what's it like to have Lucas Ridley for a brother!" Cindy said that every morning. It was her usual greeting.

"Horrible. Awful," Ginger always answered.

"Poor Ginge," Cindy would sigh.

"Can't believe you drew Ginger Bidwell for a sister!" Lucas's best friend Eddie always said as he saw the two arrive at school. "Jeez, Ginger *Bid-well*!"

And Lucas would glare at Eddie until Eddie shrugged and stuffed his hands into his pockets.

At school, the kids were in post-vacation shock.

"I can't get used to this," Lucas complained. "One minute we have all this free time and the next, we have to just sit still. How can I learn anything when I have to just—sit—still!"

"I need another Christmas vacation," Eddie said, chomping down on his sandwich in the cafeteria.

"You shouldn't talk with your mouth full," Cindy told him. "Besides, it's not Christmas vacation we need now, it's *summer* vacation. We should start summer vacation *now*."

Lucas snorted at Cindy. "Who asked you to sit down at this table and who cares what you think?" he said. "We were trying to have a conversation without you butting in."

Ginger leaned across the table. "We were here first, for your information," she said, and made a face at him. "*You* were the ones who interrupted *us.*"

"What're you, crazy or something?" Lucas cried. "We were sitting right here when you two plunked your stupid trays down and started whining at each other. Everybody knows that."

"You *jerk*, Lucas Ridley!" Cindy hollered. "You can't even see who's right in front of you before you sit down!"

Eddie swallowed hard with a gulping noise, making Ginger wince. "She's right, Luke," he said. "They're so unnoticeable, we probably sat down without even seeing 'em."

"Yeah," Lucas laughed. "They're the kind you pass right by. . . ."

"Oh, just shut up!" Ginger said, banging her fork on the plastic tray.

"Good answer, Vir-*gin*-ia," Lucas said with a grin.

"Same to you, Lucas Jer-e-*mi*-ah," Ginger answered, and stuck out her tongue at him.

"Let's just sit somewhere else," Cindy suggested. "Rita and Ellie are over there—"

But Ginger shook her head. "No way. I don't want him and his stupid friend to think they made us move. Let *them* move if they want to."

No one moved. No one spoke, either, and the only sounds at the long table were those of crackling paper lunch bags and forks scraping against plastic plates. (And Eddie's slurping the last of his milk through a straw.) Then Eddie burped, Cindy said "Gross!", Lucas laughed, and the four sat back in their chairs waiting for the bell to ring.

"Bet I know what you're doing this weekend," Eddie said as he leaned way back in his chair.

"Yeah," Lucas said, "same thing you're doing, probably."

"Yeah," Eddie said. "Probably." They slapped five and nodded conspiratorially at each other.

"What?" Cindy whispered to Ginger. "What are they doing? Do you know?"

But Ginger didn't bother to whisper back. "It's no big hot secret!" she said. "They're doing what I'm doing, too. Watching the playoffs on TV."

"The what?"

"The playoffs. The two football games."

Cindy looked blank.

"The AFC and the NFC teams are playing. You know—to see who goes to the Superbowl."

Cindy made a face. "Who cares?" she said.

"*Now* we're talking jerkville, Ginger," Lucas said. "This is your best friend?"

"Cindy doesn't like football, so what?" Ginger told him. "Your mother doesn't like it, either, and I still like her and so do you. It's a free country, y'know. Cindy likes dancing and you don't. You can't even do it."

"Dancing! Puh-leeze!"

"See? You just want everybody to be like you. Yuch!"

All four looked up at the clock. Still at least another two minutes to the end-of-lunch bell. Lucas bent down to retie his shoe. Eddie scratched his ear. Ginger folded her paper napkin into twelfths and Cindy counted the tiles on the ceiling.

"Betcha don't even know who's playing," Eddie began, but Ginger was ready. "The Rams and the Forty-niners and the Broncos and the Browns!"

The bell rang and all four sighed with relief. They grabbed trays, papers, and leftovers and headed for the door.

"Yeah," Eddie called at Ginger's retreating back, "but when does the game *start*?"

"Next time we won't sit anywhere near them," Cindy said as they dumped their trash.

"Right," Ginger agreed.

"Are you really going to watch football all weekend?"

"Just Sunday. One game at one, one at four. I love it—I just can't wait. Except always before, my dad and I watched by ourselves. Now we'll have you-know-who around, making comments, eating all the food, arguing. . . ."

"I keep forgetting you're such a sports fan," Cindy said. "We never talk about sports when we're together."

"That's because you're not a sports fan," Ginger said, and smiled at her friend. "We've got lots of other things we can talk about."

"You want me to come over and watch with you Sunday?" Cindy asked.

Ginger shook her head. "I don't think so. You don't like football for one thing and you don't like Lucas."

"Well . . . I'd rather put up with Lucas than put up with Eddie. . . . At least Lucas is cute."

"I'll never tell him you said that, Cin," Ginger said with a grin. "And I'll never make you watch football. But thanks for offering!"

Eddie and Lucas hurried down the hall from the cafeteria.

"I like having gym right after lunch," Eddie said. "You get to work it all off."

"Not all," Lucas said, and poked at his friend's rather prominent tummy.

"Hey, I'm in great shape!"

"Yeah," Lucas agreed, "if a pear is the shape you want to be."

"Aw, Luke . . ."

"Eddie, I'm just kidding. You wanna come over Sunday and watch the games with us?"

"You nuts? Watch football with Ginger Bidwell?"

"No. With me and her father. He's great. Ginger can watch the games up-stairs in her bedroom."

"Yeah, she'll love that!"

"She knows sports, though," Lucas conceded. "Y'know, she's right in there every time I try to talk sports with her dad."

"Well, you should've known about Ginger and sports before your folks got married. I mean, remember when she was the only girl on our hockey team? She was better than us even then!"

"She was not better."

"Yeah, Lucas, she was. And you know what?"

Lucas held up his hand. "Don't say it, Eddie—"

"She still is."

"I told you, *don't say it*!"

THREE

SCRIMMAGE

There really was a Tudor Lake. It was in a clearing just past Tudor Lake Park to the west. It wasn't very big, but that was fine because it froze over every winter and was great for skating!

The local Boys' Club and several of the town store owners sponsored hockey teams for all ages, and most of the town loved either to play or to watch the games.

When they were younger, Ginger and Lucas were on the same team, but for the last two years they had played against each other, with Ginger a wing on Mike's Pharmacy team and Lucas a defenseman for Eggleman's Groceries. (On the field, though, the teams called themselves the Stingrays and the Comets.)

On this January Saturday, the day before the Superbowl playoffs, several teams had arranged games down at the lake. Ginger's and Lucas's teams were to get there early for a scrimmage before the actual game.

They stood together at the front door of their house with both their parents in attendance, ready for a big send-off.

"Will you be warm enough?" Marcia asked, yanking Ginger's ski cap down over her ears.

"Go get 'em, Tiger," Arthur said, smacking Lucas on his shoulder.

"Daddy," Ginger said, "does that mean you want *his* team to win?"

"Honey, it just means that I want you

both to have a wonderful time and play as well as you can."

"Hmph," Ginger sniffed.

"And you know that's what I mean. Don't you?"

Ginger repeated her snort.

"Don't you?"

She nodded, hiking up the ski cap which Marcia mashed down again.

"Be good sports!" the parents called as the two left the house and moved off the porch together.

"Bye!" Marcia said, waving cheerily.

"We'll see you at the game!" Arthur called.

Ginger and Lucas walked side by side until they heard the front door close. Then Ginger stopped to check something on her skates and Lucas took some huge strides to put himself farther ahead.

"You're wasting all your energy!" Ginger said, loudly. "You should've jogged this morning, not right before the game!"

"I'm not jogging!" Lucas yelled

back, but his voice was lost in a gathering wind.

"What?"

"I said, *'I'm not jogging!'* "

"What?"

"Forget it!"

"Thinks he's so hot," Ginger muttered to herself. "Who cares what he said, anyway. . . . The Stingrays'll cut Lucas Ridley and his team right down this afternoon. I'll show him, you can bet on that. . . ." She wrapped a dangling scarf end over her mouth and ears.

"Thinks she knows everything," Lucas growled into his turtleneck. "Don't even have to jog to be faster than she is. . . . Even Eddie can walk faster than Ginger Bidwell. Let's see how she likes it when the Comets cream the Stingrays. She'll see who's wasting energy. . . ." His skates were dangling over his left shoulder and he clamped an elbow over one of them to keep it from bouncing against his side.

They caught up with each other at a

traffic light and arrived at the lake's community pier at the same time.

"That pass went past two lines! Any idiot knows that goal doesn't count!"

"It did not go over two lines! Besides, how would you know, you're spending most of the game on your back!"

Lucas and Ginger were nose to nose in the middle of the rink. Their teammates stood around watching them.

"Was it this bad before they got to be brother and sister?" one of the Comets asked Eddie.

"Yeah," Eddie replied, "it was always this bad. Ginger got her hair caught in Lucas's lunchbox when they were in third grade and he got a big kick out of it and that's how it's been ever since."

"I think it's worse since they got to be brother and sister."

"Yeah, I guess," Eddie said.

Ginger was yelling at the top of her lungs. "I only fell once and that's 'cause your goony friend tripped me and if this were a real game instead of a scrimmage there would've been a two-minute penalty on that one!"

"Y'know—Y'know—" Lucas stammered, "you shouldn't even be playing—"

"If you're gonna say because I'm a girl, Lucas Ridley, just watch this hockey stick remove your head!"

"Yeah, right, in your dreams! What I was about to say was, you give bad sportsmanship a bad name!"

"Oh, yeah?"

"Yeah!"

"Ridley and Bidwell, cut it out!"

Mike, from Mike's Pharmacy, had arrived. "It's almost game time," he said. Beckoning to Ginger, he added, "I want all the Stingrays right over here!"

As he took his players off to one side for a pregame pep talk, the parents, friends, and relatives of the team members began to arrive. Wearing snowboots and down jackets, carrying thermoses and blankets, they crunched through the crusty snow and made their way to the small wooden spectator stand the Lions Club had put up.

"Did you hear Mike yelling at the kids?" Arthur asked Marcia as they spread their blanket on the seat and sat down.

"Uh-huh." She sighed. "Do you think they'll ever stop, Arthur?"

"Oh, sure they'll stop. In only eight years they'll be ready for college."

Marcia smiled weakly at him. "I don't know why I come to these games all the time," she said. "I don't understand them and it's always freezing. I think they put these benches up right where the wind whips the hardest."

"You come because your children are playing," Arthur told her, "and because it makes them feel good to know you're here."

"Uh-huh," Marcia said again. "Oh, look, Arthur, you've got a rip right at the hem of your jeans."

"Yes, I do." He made a tight-lipped face. "I have a rip on the hem of every pair of pants I own, haven't you noticed?"

"Oh . . . Frank?"

"Who else has teeth sharp enough to rip through corduroy?" he asked.

"*Hey, watch that!*" Lucas yelled.

"*You* watch it!" Ginger yelled back.

"Maybe the kids do." Marcia sighed.

They walked to their car through the woods: Ginger on Arthur's left side, Lucas at his right, Marcia a few steps behind.

"I should've gotten an assist on Hubert's goal," Lucas complained. "I got it to Eddie before he got it to Hubert." He poked a finger at Ginger across Arthur's midsection.

"Oh, yeah, well you just happen to be forgetting that Willy touched the puck before Eddie picked it up for the pass. And Willy's *our* defenseman." She poked back at him, leaning over her father.

29

"Hey, you're going to trip me, you guys, cut it out!" Arthur said.

"So who's right, Daddy?" Ginger asked.

"Well, you know the rules, Luke," Arthur said, patting Lucas's back. "She's right."

"Well . . . we should have new rules, then," Lucas announced.

"Aaaaarrrrgggghhh!" Ginger yelled.

Quickly, Arthur propelled Lucas ahead of her up a hill. "Tell you what," he said, "why don't we have a Consolation Prize Pizza? We'll meet the women at home."

"All *right!*"

Ginger waited for Marcia to catch up and then she pouted a little as the two made their way out of the park.

"Boy, I would have been better off losing," she said.

"Oh, no. Look at the bright side—we drop them off at the pizza place, but we get to ride home. They have to walk. And it's getting dark. And even colder!"

"That's the bright side?" Ginger didn't mind the exercise. Marcia hated it.

"Anyway, dear, I thought you played very well. You certainly can skate!"

Ginger smiled. Marcia knew as much about hockey as Ginger knew about publishing, but she thought it was nice of Marcia to compliment her anyway.

"*I'll* tell you what," Marcia said, and put her arm around Ginger's shoulders. "While they're having pizza, why don't the two of us drop into Bigger's Department Store and see how that cute red parka with the furry hood looks on you?"

Ginger grinned up at her. She couldn't begin to guess how Marcia even knew she had admired that parka!

On Sunday, Ginger, Lucas, and Arthur spent their time watching and screaming at the television set and walking back and forth from the family room to the kitchen and bathroom.

Arthur tried to get Marcia to watch

with them, but football bored her, so she sighed a lot over the Sunday paper until the telephone rang. She went into the kitchen to answer it and then squealed.

"That squeal means it's your Uncle Marvin," Arthur said to Luke, who smiled. Marvin and Luke's Aunt Sudie lived in the Midwest. They'd come east to meet Arthur and Ginger and to be attendants at the wedding.

"They don't like me," Arthur said to Lucas.

"Nah, they just don't know you that well," Lucas replied.

"He's *fine*, Marvin!" they could hear Marcia saying. "No, really, he's a very sweet man. You just don't know him yet, that's all."

"See?" Arthur nudged Lucas.

"Lucas adores him," Marcia was saying. "We both do. And of course, Ginger's a doll!"

"Some doll," Lucas muttered.

"No, they're all watching the game,"

Marcia said. "What do you mean, *what* game?"

"Not sports fans, your aunt and uncle, are they?" Ginger whispered.

"Don't poke," Lucas told her.

"Marsh? Come on in!" Arthur called. "Come sit with us!"

"I'm talking to Marvin and Sudie!" she yelled back. "I'm still on the phone!"

Arthur sighed. "Well . . . it's nice they care so much about her . . . I guess. . . . But they call every time there's a game."

"He's only being a big brother," Marcia had said during the wedding, when Arthur complained that Marvin was sizing him up. "And anyway, he lives in Ohio, so you won't have to see him very often."

That was true, so Arthur tried not to begrudge Marcia the fun of talking all day while he and the kids watched football.

As Marcia hung up the phone, she

heard a rousing cheer from the living room.

"What is it?" she asked, hurrying in.

"It's San Francisco versus Denver!" Lucas cried, grinning from ear to ear. He looked bleary-eyed but happy.

"What is?" Marcia asked.

"The Superbowl!" Ginger told her. "The Forty-niners are playing the Broncos in the Superbowl! It's gonna be in New Orleans!"

"That's nice," Marcia said.

"It was a good day today, wasn't it?" Arthur said, smiling as he tucked Ginger into bed.

"Yeah . . ."

"What's the matter?" He smoothed her bright curls as he sat down on the edge of her bed.

"Nothing . . ."

"Aw, come on, Ginge. You're usually wired after a full day of football. Something bothering you? Let's have it."

"Well . . ." She put her hands behind her head on the pillow.

"What?"

"It's just . . . This is the first year we didn't watch the playoffs by ourselves."

"Ohh."

"And I liked it better when we watched it alone."

"Yeah, I know, honey. . . ."

"Didn't you?"

"Ginger—"

"Except maybe now you have the boy you always wanted to watch football with and you don't need me anymore. " She looked at the ceiling and away from his face.

Arthur shook his head slowly. "You know, for a smart girl, that's pretty dumb thinking."

"It is?"

"You bet it is. I love you and I love watching football with you and I love doing everything else with you, too! Having Luke around is great. He has another voice, another opinion. Makes us sit up and listen. I look at it as enhancing our family, adding something to it, not taking something away. Certainly not taking away from what I feel about you."

"Really?"

"Yeah. Really. And by the way, I would appreciate just a little . . . uh . . . less voice, opinion and personality sometimes . . . especially at the dinner table."

"Mmmmm . . ."

"Try not to fight with each other so much. It's hard on Marcia."

"Yeah . . ." Ginger mumbled. "But it would be easier if he were a girl. . . ."

"Oh, boys aren't so bad. You'll have to take my word for it for now. Meanwhile, see if you two can clean up your act."

"I'll try."

"Good. 'Night, Ginge."

" 'Night, Daddy." She didn't add—as she had been going to—that she thought that maybe she was just a little too old to be tucked in every night. Because maybe she wasn't that sure she was. . . .

FOUR

THE BIG WIN

Frank yapped and whined and whimpered as the front door opened the next night because he knew it was Marcia, coming home from work, and he was always excited to see her.

"Hi, Frankie," Marcia said absently as she bent down to pet the dog. *"Arthur? Kids?"*

Ginger was in her room. Lucas was watching television. Arthur was in the kitchen. Frank continued to say hello for all of them.

Arthur appeared in an apron to get a

dish from the dining room hutch.

"Hey!" he said with a grin. "Didn't hear you come in!"

Marcia hung up her coat. "Even with Frank making all that noise?"

"I tune Frank out. I refuse to acknowledge him. Either that or I bite his ankles back." When he gave her a kiss on the cheek, the dog chomped down on the cuff of his pants. Arthur shook him off. "How was your day?" he asked Marcia.

"Oh . . . it was okay . . . sort of. How was yours?"

"Mine was great. Three disasters that were supposed to happen, didn't happen!" He spread his arms wide in triumph.

"Terrific! Did you heat the spaghetti sauce?"

"You bet. And I added a few things. Kids! Mom's home!"

"You *added* a few things?"

"Just a few."

"Hmmmm . . ."

Ginger and Lucas burst into the kitchen with greetings and Marcia hugged both of them.

"Wash up, you guys," she said.

"What did you mean when you said your day was okay but 'sort of'?" Arthur asked as he handed Ginger and Lucas silverware for the table.

"Well, the work was okay, but . . . Did I tell you about that office contest we had?" She pulled out a kitchen chair and sat down.

"No, what contest?"

"What contest, Mom?" Lucas asked. "You didn't say anything about a contest."

"Oh. I guess it's because I was superstitious. I really wanted to win first prize, that's why I didn't say anything."

Everyone stopped what he or she was doing to look at her.

"And?" Lucas said. "Did you win?"

"Well . . . sort of." Marcia scratched her head.

Ginger jumped up and down. "That's great! That's great, Marcia! What was the prize?"

"Well . . . See, the parent company runs this contest every year. It's called their International Dream Contest, and everybody in all the divisions gets a chance to compete, and it's always the same; you write a short essay or whatever on something you think will improve the company or company relations or—" She stopped to take a breath. "And I always send something from our little newsletter because even though we're small, we do well for them and—"

"So what'd you write, Marcia?" Ginger asked.

"Never mind what she wrote, what'd she *win*?" Lucas asked.

"Lucas!"

"Sorry, Mom. What'd you write?"

"Oh, I won't bore you with it, it had to do with stock options as motivation instead of—well, anyway, the thing is I did win—"

"Great!" they all shouted.

"But it was third prize, not first—"

"Well, still!" Ginger cried.

"Yeah, and out of all those people competing!" Lucas said.

"Honey, we couldn't be prouder!" Arthur said, beaming.

"Thanks. Thanks, all of you. It's just that I really thought I had a winning idea this year and the prize was so terrific, but—"

"What was it?" Ginger wanted to know.

"First prize was an all-expense-paid trip to Paris. *France*, Arthur! A fabulous hotel, meals in all the best restaurants, sightseeing trips, a boat ride down the Seine . . ." She sighed.

"But you didn't win that," Lucas said.

Marcia shook her head sadly. "No," she said. "Arthur, you know, we never had time for a real honeymoon and I was so hoping that—"

"It's okay, honey. We'll have a honeymoon a little later, that's all—"

"And second prize was wonderful, too. . . . An absolutely *gorgeous* Persian rug. I saw pictures of it. It would have fit perfectly in the living room. . . ."

"Frank would've peed on it," Ginger said helpfully.

"Ginger would've tracked mud on it," Lucas offered.

"Okay," Arthur said, "the prizes have gone from Europe to the Far East. What's third prize? What'd you win?"

Marcia took another deep breath. "I'm not crazy about the third prize," she said. "But I would have *loved* the other two."

"Mo-om!"

"Mar-cia—"

"Well . . . it's a trip . . . here in the United States, not out of the country or anything, and it's only for a weekend."

"*What is it?*" they all bellowed at once.

"I won four tickets to the Superbowl. In New Orleans. That's the third prize."

There was a moment of stunned silence in the room, but only a moment.

Ginger looked at Lucas. Arthur looked at Ginger. Lucas looked at both of them.

"*Yaaaaaaaaaayyyyyy!*"

The scream came from all three mouths at once. It was deafening. They hugged each other as tightly as they could and jumped wildly around the kitchen. Plates rattled. Silverware clanked. Frank began to bark and snap at Arthur's ankles.

Marcia looked down at her lap. "The Persian rug was rose and blue," she said.

"We're going to the Su-per-bowl! We're going to the Su-per-bowl!" the three chanted, still bouncing up and down.

"With a little pale orange," Marcia finished wistfully.

It was the best dinner anyone could remember having. No one argued, no one complained. Ginger passed the garlic bread to Lucas and he passed the salad bowl to her. There were no rude remarks or faces made across the table. Every once in a while, they would smile at each other and at the grown-ups. It was a calm, contented mealtime.

When dinner was over, Ginger and Lucas quietly left the table and did their chores. There was no banging of dishes, dropping of glasses, snapping of dish towels. In the living room, Marcia and Arthur sat happily over their coffee.

"See how things work out?" Arthur said. "This may have been the best prize after all. The kids were nice to each other all evening."

"You're right." She nodded. "Let's hope it lasts."

Later that night, after a peaceful evening of TV watching, Ginger and Lucas climbed the stairs to their bedrooms.

"Your dad's right," Lucas said. "We didn't fight once all night."

"Yeah," Ginger agreed. "It was nice.

Aren't you excited about this trip, Lucas? I am!"

"Yeah, I can't wait! I just can't believe it! New Orleans, here we come!"

"Wait'll we tell the kids! Wait'll Cindy hears! She won't care about the Superbowl, but she'll be excited about the trip."

"Eddie'll croak! Watch his face when I break the news! You ever been there? New Orleans, I mean."

"Never. You?"

"Nope. But now we'll be there—at the Superbowl. In *person*! How about my mom!" Lucas shook his head in wonderment.

"Yeah . . . She's really great."

Lucas hit the landing with a yell. "Goooooo Forty-niners!"

Ginger tilted her head. "Forty-niners?" she said. *"Go Broncos!"*

Cindy said, "Wow, that's great."

Eddie couldn't speak for about a minute and then he choked. Lucas had to pat him on the back several times.

Their teacher, Mr. Murdoch, announced their good fortune to the whole class.

"Aren't you lucky, Luke!" his friends chorused.

"Fab-ulous, Ginge!" her friends cried.

"It's a week from Sunday!" Ellie said, and clapped her hands together. "When do you go up there? Down there? Over there?"

"It's down, Ellie, it's south," Ginger said.

"Well, when? Do you take a plane? I was on a plane once."

"Yeah, we take a plane, that's—" Lucas began.

"She asked *me*," Ginger interrupted. "*I'll* tell."

Lucas made a face at Eddie.

"Yes, we take a plane, but we go on Friday morning. That way we get to spend all day Friday and Saturday sightseeing and stuff. There's a lot to see in

New Orleans, and my dad says the food's terrific!"

"What about the tickets? Where're you sitting?" Charlie asked.

"We didn't—" Ginger began.

"He asked *me,*" Lucas said.

Ginger took a deep breath.

"We don't know exactly where the tickets are yet," he explained. "The company is mailing them to us. Mom said she'd try to find out where the seats are right away . . ."

"It doesn't matter," Cindy said. "Just going on a weekend to a southern city in the middle of winter sounds nice to me!"

Eddie looked disgusted. "It's not about 'going to a southern city'! It's about the *Superbowl*! Yay for Lucas and yay for Lucas's mom!"

"We'll be looking for you on TV, Ginger," Ellie said. "What'll you be wearing?"

"Oh gosh, Ginger!" Cindy cried. "You'll

have to go shopping and get all new clothes!"

They pounced on Marcia as soon as she arrived home from work.

"When are we going to get the tickets?" Lucas asked. "When are you going to find out where the seats are?"

"We ran right home from school to check the mail, but there wasn't anything from General Corporations at all," Ginger reported.

"Well, it's too soon to expect them," Marcia explained. "I just found out yesterday that I won. Anyway, it's only Wednesday and we're not leaving until next Friday, so we have lots of time." She leaned back against the couch and squeezed Arthur's hand. "I'm really starting to get excited about this trip," she said. Arthur put his arm around her and pulled her close.

"Aw, don't get mushy!" Lucas snapped.

"It's not mushy, Luke," Arthur said.

"We're happy because this is the first trip we'll be taking as a family. It's an honor that your mom won it and we both want it to be as memorable as possible for all of us."

"That depends on who wins," Lucas muttered.

"No, it doesn't," Marcia said. "*We* win. That's what matters."

"I feel a lesson coming on." Lucas sighed.

"No lesson. Just some more information." Marcia opened her purse on the coffee table and took out a notepad. "I talked to Bob Nelson from General this morning and he said we'll be staying at the Warrington."

"The Warrington?" Ginger asked. "Gee, that sounds fancy!"

"Well, it's a motel, not a hotel, so I don't know how fancy it is, but it's close to Bourbon Street and it's right on the river."

"Sounds nice," Arthur observed.

"Where's the *Superdome*?" Lucas wanted to know.

"I'm not sure, honey, but I don't think we'll have any trouble finding it once we get there."

"We can wear shorts!" Ginger said. "It'll be warm!"

"We'll get a weather report before we leave," Marcia said. "Now, you kids think about what you're going to bring. Remember, it's only for three days and two nights, so don't pack up your whole rooms, okay?"

"I have to bring my good-luck teddy bear," Ginger said.

"Good luck for the Broncos?" Luke sneered. "You'll need it!"

"Luke—"

"Well, I have to bring my good-luck *dog*," Lucas said. "Can Frank go?"

"Frank cannot go," Marcia said.

Frank whined.

"We'll get Mr. Nadler next door to come in and feed and walk him. Or he can stay at the vet's. They have a kennel there."

"He won't like that," Lucas said, and, as if on cue, Frank whined again.

"Serves you right," Arthur hissed at the dog.

Marcia continued. "So. We'll get all our meals, too. And if we want to hear some good jazz or something, Bob Nelson said that's taken care of. It should be a great time. Any questions?"

"Can we go to the French Quarter?" Ginger wanted to know.

"Oh, sure! Of course, we'll go to the French Quarter. And I want to see the Garden District, too. Don't worry, we'll find plenty to do. Now, how about you two setting the table and then getting a jump on your homework?"

"Luk-ee! Hi-i!"

Lucas held the phone away from his ear, then brought it back to speak into the mouthpiece. "Hello, Aunt Sudie," he said. He loved his aunt, but Arthur was right—sometimes on the telephone she sounded like a loud mouse.

"We're just so ex-cit-ed for you!" she squealed. Lucas winced.

"I guess Mom called you, huh?"

"Well, she sure did! Imagine! Winning a wonderful trip like that!"

"Yeah . . ."

"I bet little Ginger's just *thrilled*!"

Lucas looked over at Ginger, who was sitting on the couch petting Frank.

"Oh, yeah," he said with a grin. "Little Ginger's just thrilled, all right!"

Ginger looked up and stuck her tongue out at him.

"You know," Sudie continued, "your Uncle Marvin and I have never been to New Orleans. Never even been south of Pennsylvania!"

"Mmmmm . . . We haven't either," Lucas said.

"*How* many tickets did Marcia win? Four, did she say?"

"Yup. Four."

"Uh-huh . . . And of course, Arthur's going. . . ."

"Oh, yeah, he's going all right."

"Uh-huh . . . Well, isn't that just wonderful."

"Yup."

"Well, I just don't know when our poor old family's going to be getting together again. I declare, it's such a shame we're so far apart, isn't it?" Her voice was so high, Lucas wondered if Frank could hear it across the room. Dogs hear very high-pitched sounds better than humans, he knew. . . .

"Lu-cas?"

"Yes, Aunt Sudie?"

"I just wanted to tell you how happy your Uncle Marvin and I are for you and to tell you how much we both miss you, honey."

"Thank you. I miss you too, Aunt Sudie."

"Well, aren't you a sweetie to say that!"

Lucas nodded, as if she could see. I am a sweetie, he thought.

"Well, honey, take care of yourself, now, all right?"

"I will, Aunt Sudie. Bye." Lucas hung up.

"Lu-cas, honey, you're just an adorable *sweet*ie!" Ginger shrieked from the couch and burst into laughter.

"You *heard*?"

"Are you kidding? With a voice like that? I could've heard it in my *room*! Were she and your Uncle Marvin trying to squeeze in on our trip?"

"No . . ."

"They were, too. Good thing your mom didn't win six tickets."

Lucas wasn't going to let Ginger insult his family.

"They weren't trying to weasel in! They just called to say congratulations. And besides, Aunt Sudie's a regular baritone compared to your cousin Rose."

"Cousin Rose doesn't have a high voice—"

"High! Cousin Rose could break a set of crystal just saying hi to your father the way she does—'*Aaaaaa*rthur!' And besides, it just so happens, I *am* a sweetie!"

Ginger stood up and Frank slid to the floor.

"Up your nose!" she cried.

Lucas stomped toward her. "In your ear!" he growled.

They stared at each other, lips curled.

"We're not supposed to fight," Ginger said finally. "They might not take us."

"They're not home yet so they won't know," Lucas said.

"You'd tell them."

"*You* would."

"Anyway, *weasel* was *your* word, not mine. And it sounded to me like that's what your Aunt Sudie was trying to do."

Lucas tried to duck the argument by saying, "If Mom won six tickets, we'd probably take Eddie and Cindy."

"Yeah," Ginger said, brightening. "That'd be a good idea." She sat down again. "Are you sure there was nothing in today's mail?"

"Yeah, I went through it all three

times. Bills and a postcard from the vet that says Frank's due for his shots."

"Maybe they mailed the tickets to your mom's office," Ginger suggested.

"Yeah. Maybe they did. We'll check when she gets home."

The week ended with no tickets arriving, either at the Ridley-Bidwell home or at the office of Marcia's newsletter, *Womenswork.*

"Don't worry," Marcia said on Sunday night. "They'll be here. We have all week. Bob Nelson assured me they'd mailed them out. Along with the vouchers for the meals and the motel and everything."

"If we like it, maybe we could stay for Mardi Gras, huh, Mom?" Lucas suggested.

"Oh, sure. Mardi Gras's only a month later."

"I know," Lucas said.

*   *   *

Arthur stood at Marcia's elbow as she talked into the phone and took nervous little steps behind her desk.

"Well, I know, Bob, but tomorrow's Friday and we're due to leave *early,* I mean in the *morning,* and we'll miss the mail delivery and we still haven't *received* anything yet. . . ."

Arthur patted her shoulder and she ran fingers through her hair.

"I *know,* but it doesn't *help* to know that the post office is checking on it, I mean, I can't understand why you didn't send it *express.* . . . Yes, I *know* there was plenty of time. I mean, there *was* but now there *isn't* and we booked our plane tickets and . . ." She stopped talking to listen and tapped her fingernails on the desk. "Okay. Yes, okay. Well, are you sure? I mean, you're really sure, Bob, because you were sure about the letter, but we still didn't . . . okay, okay. I *said* okay, Bob, I mean, I really don't have a choice here, do I? What do you mean, I sound desperate, I'm *not* desperate, I'm *very grateful for this trip!*" She hung up.

Arthur gave her a hug. "Hey," he said. "It's all right. Whatever happens, it's not worth getting so upset about."

"You're right," she sniffed. "I'm glad you were here."

"So what did he say?"

She sat down heavily in her chair. "He said that he will call the Warrington and settle everything with them so that when we get down there, they'll know who we are and everything will be all right at that end."

"Okay . . ."

"And we should use our own credit cards for the plane fare and meals and then send all the receipts to him and he'll pay us back."

Arthur gulped. "And what else? What about the Superbowl tickets?"

"Oh, right. The tickets. I forgot about them. I'll call him back."

Arthur made a strangled noise in his throat.

FIVE

PREGAME WARM-UP

That night they were almost too excited to eat. They munched on snacks from the kitchen while they made and remade lists, organized luggage, and checked schedules.

"Okay, how's this?" Arthur asked, glancing at his notes. "Six A.M.: wake-up. Six-thirty: breakfast."

"No, wait—" Marcia called back. "I can't have breakfast ready for everyone by then. I have to shower, dress, put on makeup, get my last-minute stuff ready—"

"*We'll* get breakfast for ourselves," Arthur reminded her.

"Oh. Okay."

"Nothing fancy, just—you know."

"Uh-huh. Then at seven, you have to get Frank to the vet."

"I thought we'd decided we'd drop Frank on the way to the airport."

"Dr. Ames isn't *on* the way to the airport."

"I was thinking of Dr. Pease."

"*Why can't Mr. Nadler come and feed him, like you first said?*" Lucas called from his room.

"*Because he needs his shots and there's a kennel right there and we might as well kill two birds with one stone!*" his mother yelled. "Besides, it's only for the weekend."

"Frank *hates* the vet!" Lucas hollered.

Marcia turned to Arthur. "Shouldn't we take him to the vet he knows? I mean, don't you think he'd feel more comfortable?"

"I don't think it matters, honey,"

Arthur replied. "To a dog, a vet's a vet, right? Besides, if we take him to Dr. Pease, we won't have to go out of our way and he'll be spending less time there."

"I guess you're right. That makes sense," she agreed.

"Should I take these?" He held up a pair of yellow and green Bermuda shorts with red and orange flowers.

Marcia clamped her lips together so she wouldn't laugh.

"Or do you think they're too loud?"

"Loud?" she managed. "What makes you think they're . . . uh—" She suddenly burst into giggles.

"Yeah, too loud, maybe," Arthur said.

"What's going on in there?" Ginger yelled from her room, but the grown-ups were laughing too hard to hear her. She was choosing which T-shirts to pack when Lucas poked his head in from the doorway.

"Hey," he said.

Ginger looked up. "What?"

"Can I come in?"

"You are in," she said, and he was, having stepped over the threshhold and maneuvered himself near Ginger's dresser.

"Listen, uh . . . Can you talk to them about leaving Frank at the vet?"

Ginger tilted her head. "Why don't *you* talk to them?"

"Well—see—it's hard to explain."

"Try."

"Well, the thing is—see, Frank's *my* dog, and if *I* say anything, they'll just say, oh, what do you expect, it's his dog."

Ginger wrinkled her nose.

"Don'tcha get it, if *you* talk to them, it'll be like he's not your dog, but you really *care* about him. Then my mother will think that's so nice of you and your father won't want to upset my mother— aw, I told you it was hard to explain."

Ginger shook her head. "No, I get it. It's your sneaky way to get Frank to stay here by using the feelings of our parents to not want to hurt each other's stepchild."

Lucas grinned widely. "Yeah!" he said. "I underestimated you!"

Ginger smiled back. "Yeah, you did, but forget it. It won't work."

"Why?"

"Because Frank does need to get his shots, Lucas, and because it makes sense for him to be where he's really looked after. It's easier to leave cats by themselves for a weekend than dogs."

"You sound like some grown-up!" he told her.

"Would you really trust even Mr. Nadler to get here on time, walk him long enough, do all that stuff?"

Lucas twisted his lips. "Well . . . yeah. Why not?"

"*I* wouldn't, if it were *my* dog," she said. "He may not be happy, but I'd want him where he was safe."

"Sheesh," Lucas mumbled.

"Can I borrow your denim jacket?" Ginger asked.

SIX

RUNNING PLAY

The first arguments occurred before the sun even rose.

"Get outta the shower!" "I just got in here!" "An hour ago!"

"You used my blue bag!" "It's *my* blue bag!" *"Mine!"*

"You used up all the soap. . . ."

". . . shampoo . . ."

". . . Rice Krispies . . ."

"Stop!" Arthur yelled from the living room, Marcia from upstairs. The kids lapsed into sullen silence.

"Lucas?" Arthur called. "Where's Frank?"

Lucas looked around. "Gee, I don't know," he answered.

"You do, *too!*" Ginger whispered across the breakfast table.

"I *don't,* honest!"

"Really?"

"Yeah! Animals are very sensitive, you know. They sense things all on their own. I bet Frank's hiding somewhere."

"Did you feed him this morning?"

"No. Mom said not to because he'd throw up."

"*Frank!*" Arthur yelled. "*Frank!* He-eere, Frank!"

Lucas giggled into his glass of milk. "Go for it, Frank!" he murmured to himself. "We can always call Mr. Nadler from the airport and he'll come over and take perfectly good care of you!"

They heard Marcia's footsteps on the stairs. "Ar-thur—I've got him, honey!"

Lucas's face fell. Even Ginger sighed.

"I ducked under the bed for my slippers and there he was, cowering in a corner."

They heard the whimpering dog.

"Poor little guy," she continued. "I know he knows what's going on. You know, animals sense things people can't begin to understand."

"Told you," Lucas grumbled.

"Okay," Arthur said, "here's his carrying case. You get him into it while I collect the bags. We're running a little late, hon. *Kids! We're running late!* Get those dishes in the dishwasher and let's roll!"

"Now!" Arthur peered into the family station wagon. The luggage fit perfectly in the back—they had decided to take one small bag each, instead of larger ones combining things—and each family member was in his or her proper place: Luke in back on the left, Ginger on the right, Marcia up front next to the driver's seat.

"We have everything?"

"Yes, Daddy."

"Yeah, Arthur."

"Yes, honey."

"You *sure*?"

"Sure," Marcia said.

"Daddy, does it look like snow?" Ginger asked.

"Don't even think it," Arthur told her.

"A few stupid clouds and she thinks it's going to snow!" Lucas chimed in.

"Stop!" Marcia said. "Everything is *fine*. I just called to confirm our flight, all our stuff is here, and I gassed up the car on the way home yesterday. That should do it. Get in, Arthur."

"Right."

They pulled out of the driveway and headed out.

"What'll we do with our winter jackets?" Ginger asked. "We won't need them once we're on the plane."

"That's right," her father said, "but

we'll need them until then. It's a long ride to the airport, so just keep them on."

"And of course, we'll need them coming back on Sunday night," Marcia reminded them.

"Ooooooh, I don't want to think about that," Ginger said.

"Yeah, me, too," Lucas said. "It's just starting, I don't want to think about it's being over."

"What time was the flight, Dad?"

"Nine-twenty. We have lots of time."

Lucas said, "Don't they tell you to get to the airport at least forty-five minutes before your flight?"

Arthur looked at his watch. "Is it really twenty after eight now?" He gulped.

"No, you're five minutes fast, Dad." Ginger tapped her own watch. "Mickey Mouse says eight-fifteen."

"Well, still, Arthur. It takes at least a half hour to get to the airport—"

"Don't get upset, everyone, I said we have lots of time and we do. One half hour before flight time is plenty, and we'll make that easily."

"If there aren't any red lights, accidents, or construction work on the highway," Lucas murmured.

"Now, Luke," his mother said.

"What's that?" Ginger asked. "That—up ahead—"

"I knew it. A road guy with a flag." Lucas slapped his palm against his forehead.

"Stop it, now," Arthur warned.

"Well, *I* was ready on time," Lucas said. "Ginger had to look for her teddy bear—"

"What a lie! I packed Teddy last night—"

"*Stop, you two!*" Marcia said, and there was silence.

Following the three-and-one-half-minute delay on the road, the rest of the ride to the airport was uneventful. Arthur had the car parked in the "overnight" lot by 8:55.

"Okay, everybody out!" he said, but it was an unnecessary remark. Ginger, Lucas, and Marcia already had the tailgate down and were grabbing their bags.

"Uh-oh . . ." Lucas clamped a hand over his mouth.

"What is it?" Ginger hissed.

"Look . . ."

"Oh, *no!*" Marcia cried.

"What in heaven's name—" Arthur came around to the back of the car. "Oh, no . . ." he said weakly.

Behind all the small luggage was Frank's carrying case.

"It was because we were so rushed—I completely forgot the vet—"

"Frank was the first one in the car. Then we all threw our luggage on top of him." Marcia was clucking her tongue.

"I knew we should've left earlier," Lucas complained.

"Don't blame it on me," Ginger warned.

"Stop!" both parents yelled.

"Well, what'll we do?" Ginger asked.

Lucas beamed. "I guess we'll just have to take him with us!"

"Yap!" Frank said.

Arthur found a row of blue and red plastic seats and he told the others to *sit* and *stay* there until he had checked them all in and returned.

"Is that an order, dear?" Marcia asked sweetly.

"Not for you, of course," Arthur replied, looking a little frazzled. "But if you'd stay and keep an eye on everything, I'd appreciate it. . . ."

"Sure," Marcia agreed, "as soon as I get back from the ladies' room."

Arthur watched her go with mounting distress.

"Don't panic, Daddy," Ginger said. "We're ten. We can take care of ourselves."

"I know, I know . . ."

71

"We won't fight," Lucas said.

"You sure?"

"We're sure," Ginger said. "Go ahead, you better check us in. You need to take Frank with you?"

"Uh . . ." He looked down at the carrying case. "No, I'll come back for him. First I'd better find out what I'm supposed to do to get him on the plane. I've never flown with a dog before. The bags are small enough to carry on, so you stay here with everything."

"Okay."

"Now *watch* everything."

"Okay."

"I'll be right back."

"*Okay,* Dad."

He hurried away through the crowd.

"What's he so worried about?" Lucas asked, reaching for the pet-carrying case. "You'd think we were totally irresponsible or something." He put the cream-colored vinyl case on his lap and peered in through the long air slats. "Hi, Frankie. Isn't this great? After all that, you don't have to go to the vet, whaddya say, boy?"

Frank whined.

"Aw, you're uncomfortable in there, aren't you, fella? You weren't supposed to be in there more than a few minutes. Here, come on out and sit on my lap."

"Lucas, you better not take him out," Ginger said.

"You know what you can do with your opinions, Virginia."

"You said we wouldn't fight."

"Who's fighting?" Lucas held Frank, cuddled in his left arm, while he put the case back on the floor at his feet. "See, boy? Isn't this nicer? Look at all the people! Hey, Frankie, how'd you like to take a plane ride, huh?"

In answer to that, Frank suddenly hitched his back, squirmed once, and dug his back legs into Lucas's rib cage.

"Ow!" Lucas yelled as Frank hopped from his lap to the floor. "Frank!"

But Frank landed running, and Lucas was on his feet, too, hurtling between people's legs and luggage and calling, "Frank! Come back, Frank!"

Ginger looked wildly around. She wanted to help Lucas round up Frank, but she knew she shouldn't leave the luggage. Luckily, Marcia reappeared.

"Where's Lucas?"

"He's . . . uh . . ." Ginger could only point. The gasps and screams from their fellow travelers as either Frank or Lucas made contact with them was enough for Marcia to get the picture.

"Frank got out."

"Well," Ginger said, debating whether or not to tell, "he's not in any- more. . . ."

"And Lucas is chasing him."

"You've got that right."

"Where's Arthur?"

"Here," her husband said. He was smiling. "Everything's fine," he said, waving boarding passes.

"Think again," Ginger said.

* * *

This time, Marcia stayed with the luggage while Ginger and Arthur took off in search of Luke and Frank.

"We're going to miss the plane," Arthur said, huffing and puffing.

"We'd better not. I'll kill him," Ginger said.

"Marcia said we had six minutes to board."

"There! I see him! There he is!" Ginger grabbed her father's arm and they elbowed their way toward a news kiosk where Lucas, red-faced and almost in tears, was clutching a squirming and struggling Frank.

"I got him!" Lucas said when he spotted them. "Look, I got him!"

"Good for you," Ginger sneered. "If we miss the plane, we'll all be ever so grateful."

"We won't miss it," Arthur said. "Come on, we'll get Marcia and hurry down to gate fifteen. Let's go!"

* * *

"Buy some magazines, Arthur," Marcia said when they reached her, "and sit down. We're not going anywhere yet."

"Wh—"

"Look at Arrivals and Departures over there. It's too foggy to take off."

"Wh—"

"You can go over and ask them yourself, if you like. I just did. They'll call our flight when it clears up. Meanwhile, we're spending the first half of our vacation enjoying the sights at the airport." She closed her eyes.

"Oh, great," Arthur said, and slumped into the chair next to her.

"Terrific." Ginger sighed.

SEVEN

HALFTIME

They sat in silence on the blue and red plastic chairs.

Marcia crossed her legs and plunked her chin down on her fist.

Arthur stretched out his long legs and leaned back.

Lucas put Frank's carrying case back on his lap and held it tightly.

Ginger glowered at Lucas.

"It wasn't my fault," Lucas hissed out of the side of his mouth.

"I told you not to let him out."

"We still would've made the plane."

"I told you—"

"Stuff it!"

Arthur got up to buy a newspaper and asked the uniformed man at the desk how long it might be before they took off.

"It shouldn't be too long, sir. The fog seems to be lifting."

"Well . . . does that mean a few minutes or an hour or . . . what?"

"Probably more than a few minutes but most likely less than an hour," was the reply.

"I got no answer at all," Arthur told the others when he returned. "We might as well go eat something. Let's find a coffee shop."

"We just ate, Arthur," Lucas reminded him.

"I could use a cup of coffee," Marcia said, standing.

"I could probably go for a hamburger," Ginger said.

"A hamburger! It's quarter to ten in the morning, for Pete's sake," Lucas said. "I'm staying here."

"Oh, no you're not, young man," his mother said firmly. "We're not having a repeat of The Case of the Runaway Dog. You don't have to eat, but you're coming with us."

"Aw, rats!"

They found a restaurant which served cafeteria style.

"Well, Lucas, since you're not eating anything, you go find us a table while we stand on line with our trays," Marcia told him.

"Well . . . maybe I'll eat," Lucas said.

"I bet they serve food on the plane, too," Ginger said. "We'll be stuffed."

"It's a vacation," Arthur said. "We can pig out."

Marcia had coffee, Arthur had tea and a roll, Ginger took a burger with lettuce and tomato, and Lucas piled his tray with a bowl of chili, a salad, three pieces of bread, and a dish of chocolate pudding.

"Thought you weren't hungry," Ginger said as they carried their trays to a table.

"Yeah, but it was *there,* okay?"

They found a long table with four empty chairs. The only other people seated there were a man and a woman and a spiky-haired boy who seemed to be Lucas's and Ginger's age.

Marcia and Arthur smiled politely at the couple as they sat down. Ginger and Lucas both sized up the boy and decided to ignore him. His face seemed frozen in a permanent sneer.

"Mom, you sure our tickets'll be at the gate?"

"In our name," Marcia said for what seemed to her like the thousandth time. "Bob promised."

Lucas didn't remind her of what else Bob had promised.

"I want a Bronco's hat," Ginger said.

"Yeah, get one. It'll remind you they were also in the game."

"I love Cajun food," Marcia interrupted. "I bet it's just marvelous in New Orleans! After all, that's where it—"

"You're goin' to New Orleans?" the gentleman next to her asked. A smile lit his broad face. "That's where we're goin', too!"

"Oh." Marcia smiled back.

"Y'all got relations there?" the woman asked.

"No, we—"

"*We* do. We're visitin' family there. My husband's family."

"That's nice," Marcia said.

"I'm Winnie Burnside and this is my husband, Howland."

Arthur said, "How do you do."

"And this here's little Howland Junior!" She poked the boy in the shoulder with a long finger. "We call him Howly!"

"Howly," Marcia repeated.

Howly Burnside reached for Marcia's hand and shook it. An electric buzzer went off in her palm and Marcia jumped away with a small shriek.

"Isn't that cute!" Winnie Burnside laughed and patted Howly's shoulder. "Now, what're your names?"

Marcia looked away.

Arthur took the reins. "Well, I'm Arthur Bidwell and this is my wife Marcia Ridley-Bidwell and these are our children Ginger Bidwell and Lucas Ridley."

The Burnsides looked confused.

"Maybe we should check the board," Marcia suggested.

"Not to worry," Howland Burnside said. "They'll announce the flight and we'll hear it in here. Say, I guess what you were meaning was that this is a second marriage for you folks, isn't that right?" He beamed, proud of his understanding.

"Right," Arthur said.

"Y'all widowed? Divorced, or what?"

Marcia coughed. "I think we'd better check the board," she said again.

"Now, just sit right there, Marcia,"

Howland said, patting her arm. "You won't miss the flight, I promise. Because we're going to be right on it with you, isn't that nice?"

Under the table Ginger squeezed Marcia's hand.

"Howly, why don't you say something nice to these young people. Why, they look to be just about your age. How old're you kids, anyway?"

"Ten," Ginger answered.

"Both ten! Isn't that somethin'! Howly's ten, too, aren't you, son?"

Howly acknowledged that he was ten, too, by pinching Ginger's upper arm.

"Ow!"

"What is it, honey?"

"He *pinched* me!"

"No!" Winnie Burnside cried.

"He did! It's red here . . . look . . ."

"That other kid pinched her," Howly said and sat back, looking smug.

"How could *I* do it, I'm way over here," Lucas said.

Frank, sensing tension, growled in his case under the table.

"What you got there?" Howly asked.

Both Ginger and Lucas answered, "*Nothing!*"

"You got an animal under there, right?" Howly asked, insistently. "It's okay to tell me . . . I *like* animals. I got a pet weasel. What's yours?" He grinned a mischievous grin.

"An alligator," Lucas said.

"Really? No kidding! Alligators are great! You ever see how they tie their mouths shut with big ropes? I always wanted to do that!"

Ginger rolled her eyes.

"Hey, I bet you're puttin' me on," Howly said. "That's no alligator, is it . . ."

"I'd really be more comfortable out there in the waiting room where we can hear the flight called," Marcia said, and stood up, wiping her mouth with her napkin. "Wouldn't you?"

"Definitely!" Ginger answered.

They all hurried away from the table, Lucas grabbing his dish of pudding and a spoon.

"Would you say they were a little . . . nosy?" Marcia whispered to Arthur.

"I guess they were just trying to be friendly," he replied.

"Yeah, real friendly," Ginger said, and rubbed her arm.

"Kid's a real creep," Lucas said, looking over his shoulder. "Can't believe they're on our flight. Hope we don't have to sit next to them. . . ."

"I hope they don't spoil this weekend," Ginger said. "If that kid even looks at me funny I'm going to deck him!"

"Now, now," Arthur said. "New Orleans is a big city. We're going to the Superbowl and they're going to visit family. We'll probably never see them again."

The plane was delayed an hour and twenty minutes, but they finally got off the ground at 10:40 with many sighs of relief.

"We're on our way!" Arthur said happily. "At last!"

"Did you see that kid when he walked past us?" Ginger asked. "He was laughing. I'm going to kill him."

"You and who else?" Lucas asked. "He's a big kid."

"He's not so big. He just looked big because his hair's so tall."

"Yeah, well, if he's so easy to take, why didn't you give it to him there, in the restaurant? But no, all you did was cry 'He *pinched* me!'"

"You're looking for it, Lucas Ridley, you really are. As soon as we take off these seat belts, I'm going to—"

"Stop!" Marcia said from across the aisle. "The stewardess is coming, now behave yourselves, both of you."

"Hi!" the stewardess said, bending down. "I'm Sally. Can I get you something to drink?"

"I'd like a root beer, please," Ginger said, and Lucas added, "Me, too."

"Nothing for me, thanks," Arthur said.

"Be right back," Sally said, smiling.

"Thank you," Lucas and Ginger chorused.

"Why, you're very welcome. You two are such polite, well-behaved young people. It's a pleasure to serve you."

They looked at each other guiltily.

"There's a boy just about your age in the rear who *pinched* me as I came down the aisle just now!"

"His name is Howly Burnside," Ginger told her. "Just dump my soda on him instead of bringing it here. I won't even be thirsty anymore."

Ginger actually clung to Lucas at New Orleans International Airport when she spotted the Burnsides approaching them near the baggage carousel, where they were to pick up Frank.

"Let go of me," Lucas complained. "I

thought you were going to deck him."

"I don't want to make a scene in the airport," Ginger muttered.

"Hi-i, y'all!" Howland Burnside bellowed. "Here we all are in my home town! Welcome, folks!"

"Thank you," Arthur said.

"Nice flight, huh? Howly just loved it, didn't you, son? Anyway, we're off to Cousin Walter's! Big family reunion at his place on Sunday. Can't wait to see everybody, how 'bout you, Winnie?"

His wife beamed. "You bet, honey, but say now, I surely do hope we get to see you folks, too. Maybe we could all have a meal together, what do you say? Howly'd just love that. Bet your kids would, too!"

"Sounds nice," Arthur said with a weak smile, and Ginger kicked at his shoe.

"Where are you stayin'?"

"At the—" Arthur began, but Marcia interrupted.

"We're not sure yet. But I'm sure you folks will be busy with family. Maybe we'll see you on the flight back."

Frank yapped inside his case and Lucas whirled around to see Howly Burnside kneeling down and peering through the airslots.

"Cute-lookin' alligator," Howly said.

"Hey!"

"Don't worry . . . just having a look at the little thing." Howly sneered.

Frank growled.

"I bet he pinched Frank," Ginger whispered.

"Come on Howly, honey. Well, we'll see you," Winnie called as she and her family bustled off with their bags.

"Is Frank okay?" Ginger asked.

"Yeah . . ." Lucas had been checking and now rose to his feet. "He seems okay. I still think that kid did something. . . ."

"I hope he meets a bigger cousin at his family reunion who shows him what a pinch really is!"

"Let's go, kids," Marcia said. "We're finally off to the Warrington!"

EIGHT

EARLY WHISTLE

Arthur leaned over so that he could look the desk clerk right in the eye.

"What do you mean, only one room?"

"I'm sorry, sir, but that's what I have here on my reservations list. General Corporations booked you, isn't that right?"

"Yes," Marcia said through clenched teeth. "But we were supposed to have two rooms. Bob Nelson promised."

"He's good at that," Lucas muttered.

"Honest, ma'am, you're real lucky to

have this room, your friend callin' so late and all. This is Superbowl Weekend, you know, and we're just packed. The whole city's booked up."

"Thank you," Arthur said. "We'll be okay." He turned to his wife. "I'll take one of the beds with Luke and you take the other with Ginge."

"Swell," Lucas sighed.

"Great," Ginger said.

"Perfect," Marcia growled.

"We don't need a bellboy, we can carry our own—"

"Excuse me, sir, is that an animal with you?"

"Uh—"

"Because we don't allow animals, sir. I'm sorry."

Lucas looked stricken.

"It's *not*," Ginger said quickly. "It's our bowling balls."

The clerk narrowed his eyes at them. "Your bowling balls need *air* holes?"

"No, no, it *is* a pet-carrier," Ginger

said, "but there's no pet in it. . . ." She pushed it at Lucas who headed for the stairs with it. "We just don't have a regular case to carry the balls, so we just use the pet-carrier. It's lightweight, you know."

The clerk shook his head. "Maids better not find a pet in the room. It really is against the rules."

"They won't find anything," Ginger said as they followed Lucas to the stairway.

"What room is it?" Marcia asked, holding the wrought-iron railing."

Arthur looked at the key.

"Twenty-four. What'll we do about Frank?"

"We'll have to take him with us when we go out," Ginger said. "We have no choice."

"Not to the game! Maybe I can talk to someone. I don't like breaking rules."

"I don't either," Marcia said, "but there's no other room in the city of New

Orleans and if we get thrown out, we'll be sleeping on the trolley for two nights."

"We'll think of something," Arthur said. "There's the room—Luke's standing in front of the door."

They let Frank out of the case. He growled at Arthur, shook himself, and looked around.

"He's normal," Arthur said.

"He's thinking the same thing I am," Marcia said. "Is this the best General could do?"

The room was big enough but it looked a little seedy. There were brown water stains on the ceiling; the wallpaper had faded from pink and yellow to orangey beige; one of the beds had a headboard but the other didn't; the imitation Oriental rug on the floor was threadbare. There were French doors with missing panes opening onto a small balcony.

"But we've got a TV," Lucas noted.

"Let's see if it works." Ginger turned it on. "It's a little fuzzy but it's okay."

Frank went to the door and scratched.

"Uh-oh . . ."

"Now what?" Marcia asked.

"Don't worry," Ginger said. "I already thought of this. We're on the second floor, right?

"Well, if we get some clothesline, we can make a harness and lower Frank down from the outside balcony." She went outside and peered over the edge. "See? We're in the back. There's nothing down there but a parking lot. And one of us will be down there to walk him once he lands."

"I don't like this, Ginger," Arthur said.

"Okay." Ginger folded her arms. "You think of something."

Arthur sighed. "Wasn't there a five-and-ten or some kind of store like that next door to the hotel? You can probably get some clothesline there. . . ."

"Good thinking, Dad," Ginger said.

Frank scratched again.

"But wait," Marcia said. "What do we do for now?"

"For now? Didn't you buy a newspaper before we came down here, Daddy?"

"Thanks, Ginger," Lucas said as they went down the stairs together.

"You're welcome."

"That was real good thinking."

"I know."

"So I guess I owe you one. . . ."

"I guess you do."

Lucas stuffed his hands into his pockets as they went through the front door of the Warrington Motel. "Where was that store?" he asked.

"I think it was right next door. Yeah! There it is, see? One of those big stores that sells everything . . ."

"Good thing it's right here," Lucas said. "This street is swarming with people. We'd never find anything!"

"Just feel it!" Ginger cried, holding her arms out. "The air!"

"Yeah." Lucas smiled. "It's warm. What do you think it is, about seventy?"

"At least!"

"This is great, isn't it?"

"Great!"

"What took you so long?" Marcia asked when Lucas and Ginger returned.

"Are you kidding? It was a mob scene in the store!"

"Already? It's only Friday. . . ."

"It's The Weekend, Mom," Lucas said. "Superbowl Weekend! The people are going nuts!"

"Besides, we liked the weather," Ginger added.

"I'll bet you did," her father said with a grin. "Let's go get some of it."

"First we'd better feed and lower Frank," Ginger reminded them. "Aren't we smart, Lucas and I? We remembered to buy dog food, too!" She opened the bag she was holding and took the things out.

"We're not that smart," Lucas said. "We forgot a bowl."

"We'll use an ashtray," Marcia suggested.

"The maids won't be cleaning until tomorrow," Arthur said, "so I guess it's safe to leave Frank for a while. But I don't like this at all. . . ."

"Me, too, honey," Marcia said, "but the kids are right. We really have no choice."

While Frank ate, Lucas fashioned a harness with the clothesline and slipped it over Frank's short body. "Go on downstairs, Ginger," he told her. "I'll lower him down to you."

"Fine, then we'll go enjoy some of New Orleans," Marcia said. She had changed into a pretty blue cotton dress and sandals.

Arthur, too, had changed. He wore a short-sleeved sport shirt and slacks. "Before we take in any sights," he said, "let's go over to the Superdome and make sure our tickets are there."

"Oh, you and that game," Marcia grumbled.

"Mo-om! Guess why we're *here*!" Lucas said, and his mother laughed.

The lower-Frank-to-the-ground plan worked perfectly. The dog cooperated as if he were in on the unusual procedure from the beginning, and once down, Ginger walked him along the edge of the back parking lot. Then Lucas pulled him up.

"I thought of how funny it'd be if the people in the room below us looked out their window as Frank was going by," Ginger laughed when she returned to the room. "But all the curtains were closed."

"Good. When we let him out again, it'll be night and much harder to see him."

"We're wasting our weekend!" Marcia said, grabbing her husband's arm. "Come on, guys, let's go!"

* * *

They got directions to the Superdome from the desk clerk. The stadium was definitely not within walking distance.

"Let's take a trolley!" Arthur said. "It'll be fun!"

There were so many people in the streets that it was hard to see the sights as they rode the streetcar.

"All they're talking about is *football*," Marcia complained. "I know, Lucas, 'it's why we're here.' I keep forgetting. . . ."

"Don't worry, honey, the game's not until Sunday. We'll see a lot before then," Arthur reassured her. "Speaking of seeing things, where's the camera?"

"I've got it," Lucas said. "It's safe, hanging from my neck here."

"Okay, Luke, but get ready to hand it over when we see something we really want to remember."

The ticket clerk was polite but baffled. "Ridley? I'm sorry, I just can't find anything with the name Ridley. . . ."

"Try Ridley-Bidwell," Marcia said, beginning to get anxious.

"Uh, nope . . ."

"Try *Bidwell!*" Arthur yelled.

"Uh-uh . . ." The clerk shook his head.

"Look, my wife won these tickets in a competition conducted by a highly respectable business firm, General Corporations. . . ."

"Oh, yes sir, I've heard of General Corporations."

"Well, they promised these tickets would be taken care of. We were supposed to get them in the mail, but something got fouled up and—oh, never mind, just keep looking, will you?

The clerk did, but found nothing.

"Is this something we want to remember, Arthur?" Lucas asked, holding up the camera.

"Listen, I want to talk to the promotions manager," Marcia said.

"Sure," the clerk said obligingly, happy to turn the situation over to someone else. He spoke on the phone for a moment and then pointed to a door. "Go right on up there," he said. "Mr. Hannibal's waiting for you. Third door on your left."

Mr. Hannibal turned out to be the promotion manager's assistant. He was young and bald and sweating slightly.

"Hello," he said, and shook hands with Arthur. "Awfully busy weekend, as you can imagine."

Arthur nodded. Marcia explained the problem as calmly as she could. "And," she finished, "I'll be happy to call the corporation's offices at my expense so you can talk to Bob Nelson."

Mr. Hannibal said that would be fine, but he would be glad to pay for the call. Marcia wished he would call collect.

While Mr. Hannibal spoke to Bob Nelson, Arthur paced the office. Ginger and Lucas walked in their own small circles. Marcia tapped fingernails on Mr. Hannibal's desk. She wasn't as upset about the game as the others, but she was angry on principle. After all, a promise is a promise!

Mr. Hannibal hung up. "Mr. Nelson explained it all to me, Mrs. Ridley—"

"It's Ridley-Bidwell."

"Of course, Mrs. Ridley-Bidwell. And I'm very sorry you people have been through this. I'm sure it's very frustrating. . . ."

"To say the least," Arthur said.

And Ginger added, "Yeah."

"I'm sure it can all be straightened out, once my boss gets back from his business lunch—"

"Your *boss*?"

"Well, you see, I'm the assistant promotions manager. The promotions manager, Mr. Grapehew, is out to lunch."

Arthur looked at his watch. "Excuse me, Mr. Hannibal," he said, "but it's close to four o'clock your time—"

"Our time's an hour behind," Marcia explained.

"Yes, I know—"

"Anyway, even *I* get back from lunch before four o'clock," Arthur continued. "Don't you think as his assistant *you* could handle it?"

"I'm sorry, Mr. Ridley-Bidley—"

"That's *Bidwell.*"

"Of course. Mr. Bidwell. Actually, I could explain things to Mr. Grapehew, but I was only thinking of your peace of mind, having it straightened out with him, as it were."

Arthur looked sheepish. "Sure," he said. "Sorry. We'll wait."

NINE

INTERFERENCE

They grumbled all the way back to the hotel on the trolley.

"Five-thirty!" Marcia kept saying. "And now I'm just too tired to do anything but put my feet up and lie down."

"I know, honey," Arthur said. "I'd feel better if we had at least gotten to meet Mr. Grapehew, but—"

"But he never got back from lunch. That's what happens on Superbowl Weekend." Lucas sighed. "I wonder when he'll start dinner?"

"Well, the one good thing," Ginger commented, "is that Mr. Hannibal felt so bad for us, he said he'd be sure to see that everything got fixed. He said he'd do it personally."

"Mmmmmm, so did Bob," Arthur noted.

"We didn't see anything except the inside of an office!" Marcia wailed.

"At least we saw the Superdome," Ginger said to Lucas. They had left the office during the wait and wandered around.

"Yeah. It was weird to see it empty. Can you just imagine what it's going to look like on Sunday with all those thousands and thousands of people in it?"

They climbed off the trolley into the mob on the street.

"I can imagine," Marcia said, fighting her way to the curb. "They say this city is beautiful, but all I can see are other people. . . ."

It was six-thirty by the time they

reached the front doors of the Warrington Motel. Marcia leaned against
Arthur's shoulder for support.

"I know how you feel, honey," Arthur
said, "but we'll rest up awhile, take a
shower, and then we'll all go out for a
nice dinner somewhere. How does that
sound?"

"Great." Marcia looked up and smiled
at him. They had sampled some craw-
daddies from a vendor on the sidewalk
but that was all they'd eaten since the
plane trip.

"Uh-oh . . ." Ginger's voice was so
small only Lucas heard it.

"Now what?" he asked.

Ginger didn't answer, but gestured toward the front desk.

"Uh-oh," Lucas repeated.

"We couldn't be wrong, could we?"
Ginger asked.

"No way. They're right there before
our very eyes: the lovely Mrs. Burnside,
the large Mr. Burnside, and our favorite
traveling companion—"

"Howly Burnside. Boy, Lucas, what are they doing here? I thought they were going to Cousin Walter's house for a family reunion?"

"Maybe Cousin Walter couldn't stand them either," Lucas said. He was about to whisper to his mother and Arthur to get to the stairs or elevator quickly, but it was too late. Winnie Burnside spotted them as she turned from the desk.

"Well, I declare!" she squealed as she pounced on them. "Howland, looky here! Look who it is! It's the Biddles!"

Arthur and Marcia were too stunned to correct them. They could only stare. Ginger glared at Howly who grinned back and slipped away from the group.

"There wasn't enough room for everyone at Cousin Walter's," Howland was explaining, "so he was smart enough to rent some rooms around town for the spillover. If he hadn't thought of that months ago, we wouldn't have a place to stay, what with this being the Superbowl and all. Just dumb luck that we ended up at the Warrington, right where you folks are stayin'!" He clapped Arthur on the shoulder.

"Dumb luck," Marcia said.

"Now, we were just about to plan a nice dinner in the city here. How about we all go together? We know a perfectly marvelous place. We just won't take no for an answer!"

Arthur was holding Marcia up by this time.

"Thanks, folks, really," he said, "but we're just exhausted from the day. We thought we'd just come downstairs here and eat in the Warrington dining room."

Marcia groaned.

"No, we want to show you the town!" Howland boomed, and clapped Arthur on the back, so hard he began to cough.

"Thanks anyway," Marcia said, "but we'd be more comfortable here than fighting the crowds in the streets—"

Howland shrugged and looked at his wife. "Well, Winnie, if that's what they want, why I guess we can be hospitable and stay right here with 'em, what do you say?"

"Oh, no!" Arthur protested. "We wouldn't hear of it. You go out, enjoy yourselves, after all, you're back home now—"

"No, no, our minds are made up. You're the new folks, we're the hosts— we'll stay right here with you."

Marcia leaned back against Arthur just as Howland smacked him on the back again to show his good will.

Ginger tugged at Lucas's sleeve. "Come on," she said.

"Where?"

"Just come with me."

"You're a bigger pest than Mr. Burnside," Luke complained, but he followed her a few steps. "Where are you dragging us?"

"Where'd Howly go?" she whispered.

"I dunno." Lucas looked around. "In there?"

"The dining room?"

"I think so. . . ."

They crept over to the door.

"Yeah, it's the dining room, all right. Not too many people in there now, are there?"

It was, in fact, fairly empty-looking for six-thirty. Several couples and one family were the only ones seated at tables.

"I guess it's early," Ginger said. "People must be out celebrating or something and they plan to eat later, like us. Do you see Howly?"

Lucas nudged her and pointed. Howly Burnside was at one end of the dining room looking furtively around. "What's he doing?"

"Shhh. Watch."

Howly was moving quickly and quietly from empty table to empty table. It was hard to see what he was up to because he managed to keep his back to anyone near him. Waiters in white shirts and black pants seemed to pay no attention to him as they hurried by with trays filled with water glasses and fruit cups.

"He's changing stuff," Lucas said suddenly.

"He's what?"

"He's changing stuff! Look, he's dumping salt into the sugar bowls. He's putting pepper in the sugar. He's mixing up all the spices and stuff on the tables."

Ginger stared. "I knew he was up to something sneaky. He had that smirk on his face."

"What a creep. Bet he thinks that's real funny. You'd think he'd care that his own parents would use this stuff when they eat here."

"They're not eating here. Or at least he didn't think they were. They said they were going out. They wouldn't be around when everybody used this stuff."

"That's right. . . ."

"Lucas, I've got an idea."

"What?"

"Take his picture."

"Huh?"

"You've still got the camera around your neck, haven't you? Get his picture! Hurry!"

Lucas looked at her admiringly for the second time that day. "Awright, *Ginge!*" he said. He held up the camera, aimed, and snapped.

"More, take more," Ginger said.

Lucas snapped and snapped. "This may be something we want to remember," he said.

It wasn't a fancy or formal dining room, but the Ridley-Bidwells dressed up anyway. Marcia wore a flowered print cotton sundress. Arthur and Lucas donned jackets and ties in spite of the heat, and Ginger wore a pink jumper and white blouse.

"I tried," Arthur said.

"I know." Marcia reached up and gave him a kiss. "There was no way to avoid it. This whole day has been a disaster.

We might as well just get it over with."

"At least it worked out with Frank," Lucas said brightly.

They had lowered him to the ground before they came down to dinner. This time, Lucas walked him and he seemed at home and contented. No one had seen them.

"So far," Arthur said. "Just be careful you don't lower him down onto the Burnsides' car."

"I'd like to lower him on Howly's head," Ginger said.

Just then, as if on cue, the three Burnsides appeared in the dining room doorway. Howly looked a little uncomfortable, Ginger decided.

"Hiii-ii, folks!" Howland yelled across the room. "Here we are!"

Lucas winced.

There was one empty table on the other side of the Ridley-Bidwells, and Howland Burnside grabbed at its corners and slid it along the floor until the

113

two tables nearly touched. "There we are!" he boomed. "Isn't this cozy!" The Burnsides scraped their chairs out and flopped down.

And then the dining room turned into a horror movie with a kaleidoscope of award-winning special effects.

A woman at the next table began to sneeze. When she couldn't stop, her dinner companion jumped up to help her. He bumped into a waiter with a tray of tomato bisque that spilled down the back of a gentleman at another table. Howland Burnside sugared his fruit cup with pepper and bellowed about it. A woman squeezed hot sauce instead of mayonnaise onto her lettuce and waved angrily for the waiter. A busboy slipped in the spilled soup, slid across the floor, and skidded into two diners who were paying their check. One of them screamed and fell on top of the busboy. The sneezing woman raced blindly for the ladies' room, hurtling into a waiter with a tray full of baskets containing rolls, all of which were flung into the air. The rolls bounced around the dining room like big brown hailstones.

"I declare!" Winnie Burnside exclaimed as a roll bounced off her head. On the floor, spilled sugar mixed with tomato soup that slid into puddles of mustard and mayonnaise topped with salt and pepper and squashed packets of margarine and cheese. The kitchen staff came out into the dining room to gawk, looking as horrified as all the patrons.

Ginger glanced over at Howly Burnside, who had his hand clamped over his mouth.

"Listen, what do you say we order from room service and call it a day?" Arthur said, getting up.

"Can't believe this!" Howland was yelling. "Can't believe this shoddy treatment! I'm suing, you hear? I am suing!"

Winnie was patting her husband's arm. "Now, dear."

"Don't you 'now, dear' me! This is the worst, the shabbiest—*Where's the manager! I want to see the manager of this zoo!*"

He lurched away from the table, followed by Winnie. Unseen by anyone but Ginger, Howly deliberately knocked over his water glass as he rose to follow his parents. It fell over on Marcia.

That night it didn't matter whether they had one room, two rooms, or even a suite apiece! Ginger Bidwell, Lucas Ridley, Marcia Ridley-Bidwell, and Arthur Bidwell went to bed on the second floor of the Warrington Motel on Friday night of Superbowl Weekend in New Orleans, Louisiana. Each of them was asleep the very second his or her head touched a pillow. And each of them stayed that way until morning. Not one of them moved. Not one of them even dreamed.

TEN

BLITZ

"I slept like a *rock*, did you?" Marcia asked Arthur.

"I sure did."

"I did, too. Do you think it's the air?" Ginger asked.

"Boy, I don't know," Lucas said, "but I don't remember ever sleeping that soundly!"

Marcia had already dressed and was looking out over the balcony. "It's another beautiful day," she told them, "so I'm glad we all got such a good night's sleep. We'll have the whole day for sight-seeing!"

Lucas was pouring a packet of dog food into Frank's ashtray. "What about the Burnsides?" he asked. "Will we have to go with them?"

"No, no," Arthur assured him. "Today there was a party or something at Cousin Walter's for the family. But before that, Howland was seeing some lawyers about suing the motel."

Ginger glanced quickly at Lucas. "He's not really going to sue, is he?"

"Oh, he was very serious," Arthur said. "He was pretty angry that things got so mixed up. He called the kitchen staff incompetent and a whole lot of other nasty names."

"Is he moving out, then?" Marcia asked.

Arthur chuckled. "No, he can't do that. There's not another place open in the city."

"That's right," Marcia said, "I forgot."

"I'm going to call about our tickets and make sure everything's all right before we go out." Arthur picked up the phone.

"I'm taking a shower!" Lucas cried, and bounded toward the bathroom. Then suddenly, he stopped and looked over at Ginger, who was sitting in her bathrobe on the bed. "Uh . . . you wanna use it first?" he asked.

They were ready. Ginger in a denim skirt and T-shirt; Lucas in a T and striped shorts; Arthur in chinos and a polo shirt, and Marcia in white jeans and a red blouse.

"I can't wait," Marcia said, snapping her purse shut. "Have we forgotten anything? The camera?"

"I've got it," Lucas said. "I don't mind being in charge of the camera." Ginger grinned at him. "Are you sure," he added, "that everything's okay with the tickets?"

"Well, I couldn't get Mr. Grapehew again, but Mr. Hannibal said he talked to him and that everything's okay. When we get to the gate tomorrow, the tickets will be there in our name. Or one of our names."

"Yeah, Arthur, but everyone said that before," Lucas reminded him.

"I've got a feeling this time it's all right. Mr. Hannibal seemed on top of it. He was very reassuring."

"Good."

"Now, how about some breakfast before we go out on the town? I've heard about these terrific puffy doughnuts they make here, with sugar and—"

"Now, Arthur, your waistline. . . ." Marcia patted it.

"No calorie-counting on vacation," Arthur said.

They laughed as they headed for the door, but before they reached it, there was a knock.

They all looked at each other.

"Hide Frank," Lucas whispered.

"*Where?*" Ginger cried.

"Lower him down, quick!"

"But we just lowered him!"

"Lower him again!"

"Who is it?" Marcia sang out, and to Arthur she whispered, "What'll we do if it's the Burnsides?"

"Guess whooo-oooo?" came a voice behind the door.

Arthur looked at Marcia. "It can't be," he said.

"It is. No one else sounds like that," Marcia said. She went to the door and flung it open. "Sudie!" she cried. "Marvin!"

Exuberantly Sudie and Marvin threw their arms around Marcia. They seemed to be laughing and crying at the same time.

"Well, now, aren't you surprised?" Sudie cried. "That's all we wanted to do—surprise you!"

"We're surprised," Arthur said.

"We just had to do it," Marvin said. "As soon as we heard about that trip you won, we knew we just had to be here to share it with you. Sis, you certainly are a sight for sore eyes!"

"Oh, Marvin, you, too . . ."

"But where are you staying? You know, there aren't any rooms to be had in town this weekend," Arthur said.

Marvin's eyes twinkled. "Were you surprised when they only had you down for one room when you checked in?"

"Well, yes," Marcia said. "We were supposed to have two. . . ."

"Uh-huh! Well, everything else was booked up solid, so we called here and told them to save that room for us and not to tell you. We knew you wouldn't mind the surprise!"

"You what?"

"We took that extra room. We knew you'd be so thrilled that we could all be together—we're right smack across the hall!"

"I am—I'm just so excited," Marcia exclaimed. "This is just wonderful! And aren't the rooms nice? I mean—the view! Why, we have a balcony and you can see the most beautiful gardens and flowers beyond the parking lot. Oh, Sudie, Marvin, I'm so glad to see you!"

Balcony! Lucas snapped his fingers. "Ginger?" he called when he found his voice.

"What?"

"You can pull Frank up now. . . ."

They all had a quiet breakfast in the dining room. Everyone was relieved to see the sugar in the sugar bowls and the salt and pepper in their respective shakers.

Ginger and Lucas explained their idea to their parents, who frowned a lot about it.

"But *why* do you want to stay here?" they asked. "Don't you want to see any of the city? The game is at three o'clock tomorrow, so we won't have that much time to do anything then."

"We know," Ginger said, "but we'd rather stay. There's a pool here, and video games."

"You can do that at home."

"You guys go ahead," Lucas insisted. "Looking at gardens with four grown-ups isn't my idea of fun. We'd just get lost in the shuffle."

"You wouldn't, honey," Marcia said, ruffling his hair.

"Go, Mom," he said. "Enjoy your reunion with Uncle Marvin. We'll have a better time here, won't we, Ginge?"

"Yeah," she said, "I think we will."

"You won't fight if we leave you alone together, will you?"

Ginger shook her head. "I don't think so," she answered.

They went back upstairs and put on bathing suits with shorts and shirts over them. They made sure that the Do

Not Disturb sign was still hanging from their door so that the maids who cleaned the rooms wouldn't bother with theirs. Arthur had given them some quarters to use for the games, so they were just about ready for their own vacation day.

"Too bad Arthur took the camera," Lucas said. "You never know when it might come in handy."

"Well, he said he wanted to finish up this roll and get it developed right away so he could start another one. He loves taking pictures."

"Yeah, me, too," Lucas said.

At the pool, Lucas slapped his forehead with the palm of his hand. "Oh, no!" he cried. "It's Howly Burnside again—and he's all by himself this time, just like us!"

"No! Let's go to the game room first and maybe he won't see us."

But Howly was already waving to them.

"Hey, now I have someone to hang with!" he said as he approached them. He slapped Lucas on the back heartily. "My folks are seeing a lawyer about suing the place," he said, and laughed. "I don't blame them, y'know? People could've gotten hurt last night. Come on, let's go swimming!"

They lasted in the pool for about a half hour. Ginger and Lucas got tired of being ducked and splashed and the one time they finally ganged up on Howly, the pool's lifeguard blew his whistle and made them get out of the water. They felt safer in their room until Howly left for Cousin Walter's with his parents.

"Why didn't you tell him we knew about what he did in the dining room?" Ginger asked Lucas. "Each time I started to say something, you kicked me!"

"I want to show him those pictures," Lucas said. "It will be so much better if we have them in our hands when we tell him. Especially since his father's making such a big deal out of it."

"Yeah," Ginger said, "maybe so."
Frank whined.

"He's bored," she said. "He wants to be out in the nice weather, too. I know what—let's both take him for a walk. You lower him down. I'll catch him and wait for you."

"Okay," Lucas said. "Frank will like that."

Ginger bounced down the stairs to the parking lot and stood under their balcony. "Okay," she called up, and laughed to herself as she watched the four legs and wagging tail being lowered over the railing. "He really does like it!" she cried. "He's really getting used to it! We ought to try walking him this way when we get home!"

"Yeah, you should," a voice at her shoulder said. "Because when the motel finds out you got an animal in your room, you'll be home a lot sooner than you thought." Howly Burnside leered at her.

* * *

Panic gripped both of them as they stood together in the parking lot clutching Frank's rope leash.

"This is just something else for my father to add to his lawsuit," Howly chuckled. "Keeping dirty animals in the rooms! Haw, haw!"

Ginger made her hands into fists, but Lucas held her arm.

"I think you might want to wait before you told anyone about Frank, Howly," he said.

"Yeah? Why would I want to do that?"

"Because it would be in your own best interests, that's why. There's something we could tell about you, if you tell about us."

"Oh, yeah?" Howly sneered. "What would that be?"

"You could just say it has to do with your father's lawsuit," Lucas told him.

For a moment, Howly looked confused. Then he looked angry. "What're you talking about?" he asked.

"Never mind. Meanwhile," Lucas said, "you keep your big mouth shut or you'll really be sorry."

"How-ly! Oh, How-ly! Why, there you are, darlin', we're all ready to go to Cousin Walter's now. Your daddy's finished with his meeting. Well, if it isn't the little Ridwell children. You and Howly having fun together?"

"Lots of fun, Mrs. Burnside," Ginger said.

"Well, good. Y'all can play together again maybe later this evenin' when we get back. Say bye now, Howly."

"Bye now," Howly said.

They watched him drive off with his parents.

"I never saw anyone so mean," Ginger said.

"Yeah, he's mean, all right," Lucas agreed.

"Even *you* aren't that mean," Ginger said.

"*Me?* Are you kidding? *Me?*"

"Yes," Ginger said.

"Huh?"

"Yes, I'm kidding."

The day got better. Ginger and Lucas walked Frank, then they went back to the pool and played pinball and other games in the game room. They had the Warrington pretty much to themselves, because the rest of New Orleans was out celebrating Superbowl Weekend.

Marcia and Arthur with Marvin and Sudie in tow arrived back at the motel at around four. Sudie's neat hairdo had come down around her ears. Marvin's tie was undone. Marcia had mud splatters on her white jeans, and Arthur kept mopping his face with a big handkerchief.

"Arthur," Lucas said, but Arthur had sunk onto the bed.

"Get that air conditioner on," Arthur said weakly.

"It's just beautiful, here, really," Sudie

said, fanning herself with a magazine.

"It is, isn't it, honey?" Marvin agreed. "Don't you just love it, Marcia?"

"I love being warm when I know everyone's freezing back home, don't you, Arthur?"

Arthur grunted. His eyes were closed.

"Arthur," Lucas said again, but his mother interrupted. "You kids just can't believe how crowded everything was! The Vieux Carré, the French Quarter, all the shops! The only things I got a good look at were some barges on the Mississippi. And a conga line made up of people dressed like bears."

"They weren't bears, honey, they were Broncos," Arthur said. "The Denver Broncos."

"They looked like bears," Marcia said.

"Arthur," Lucas tried again, but Sudie grabbed him from behind and gave him a big hug.

"I certainly have missed you, Lucas, honey," she said. "And we'll hardly see you this weekend. Tomorrow you'll be at that stupid football game."

"Oh, Sudie, I know," Marcia sighed. "I just wish we had more time together. But I guess we have to see that game. . . ."

"We sure do," Arthur said from the bed.

"The snapshots," Lucas said to Ginger. "*You* ask him."

"Dad," Ginger said.

"What time's your flight home tomorrow?" Marvin asked.

"Around nine," Arthur said. "We'll have to go to the airport right from the game."

"Oh, you'll be getting home so late," Sudie wailed. "Why not just stay over another night and we will too! Won't that be fun?"

Marcia said, "Yes!" At the same time Arthur said, "No!" Then Marcia and Arthur glared at each other.

They found a restaurant noted for its Creole cuisine and silently sampled pompano en papillot and crepes suzette soufflé. Ginger said, "Mmmmmm!" once and Lucas tried a "Great!" but Arthur and Marcia just glowered at each other. Sudie and Marvin smiled, seeming not to notice the tension.

"Ask him," Lucas urged Ginger, and finally, as they were leaving, she said, "Daddy, did you develop that roll of film today?"

"What roll of film?"

Lucas's heart sank.

"Oh, you did, Arthur, don't you remember? You brought it to that drug store that promised it would be ready in an hour," Sudie said.

"Oh, that's right."

"But you forgot to pick it up."

"That's right, too," Arthur said, biting each word. "I'll have to get it in the morning. I'm sure they'll be open."

Ginger grabbed Lucas. "What'll we do?" she asked.

"Don't worry. Howly'll be at Cousin

Walter's tonight. He'll be back late. When he bothers us in the morning, we'll have them."

"Let's go hear some jazz," Sudie cried.

"Yes, let's go someplace," Marcia and Marvin chorused.

ELEVEN

SUPERBOWL SUNDAY

The next morning, Arthur seemed glad to have an excuse to run out to the drugstore for the pictures. Marcia hadn't asked about staying over another night, but he thought she'd start at any minute. He understood that she didn't see her brother too often, but he didn't know who was more overwhelming—the Burnsides or Marcia's brother and Sudie.

Ginger and Lucas stayed in their room at the Warrington, pacing nervously.

They had lowered Frank already without incident, but to Lucas that only meant that good ol' Howly was just biding his time.

"Maybe he's staying at Cousin Walter's," Ginger suggested. "Maybe there was room."

"Even if there was room, they wouldn't want him," Lucas answered. "No, believe me, he'll be here. He wants to see us kicked out of the Warrington; he won't give that up."

There was a knock on the door.

"It's Marvin and Sudie," Marcia called from the bathroom.

"No, it's not," Lucas muttered, and it wasn't. It was Howly Burnside.

"Hi, there," Howly said with an evil grin. "Did you have a nice time last night? Bet you didn't eat in the dining room, did you?"

"No, we—"

"My father said no one should ever eat down there again."

"Howly—" Lucas began to pray hard for Arthur's quick return.

"We had a nice time at Cousin Walter's," Howly went on. "Some of the ladies hung their underwear in one of the bathrooms after they washed them and guess what? They all disappeared from that bathroom and were found in the magnolia trees outside in the yard. Right near the tent. And the band."

"How did they get there, Howly?" Ginger asked sweetly.

"I'm sure I can't imagine. How's your little dog?" Howly knelt down and whistled through his teeth. Frank came bounding over.

At the same time, Arthur walked in.

"Arthur!" Lucas breathed. "I'm so glad to see you. You got them!"

Arthur was holding one of the yellow envelopes that stores use for pictures and negatives. "Yes, I got them, Lucas, but—"

"Never mind!" Lucas grabbed for

them. "I'll tell you later. Come on out in the hall, Howly!" He shoved the big boy backward. At the same time he pushed Frank back into the room with the side of his foot. Then he closed the door. Even Ginger had been shut inside and she didn't dare try to follow.

"You're not going to tell about Frank, Howly," Lucas said calmly.

"Why not?" Howly was still grinning.

"Because"—Lucas held up the envelope of snapshots—"in this envelope, I've got pictures I took on Friday night after we got back from the Superdome. And you know what the pictures show?"

Howly shook his head.

"They're pictures of you. In the dining room downstairs. I had the camera, and I took them because I saw what you were doing, changing the mustard and sugar and ketchup and all that stuff. All that stuff your father's making such a big deal about, *you* did. Now, wouldn't your father like to see these pictures, Howly?

Don't you think he would?" He waved the envelope under Howly's nose and the boy backed away. His grin had disappeared.

"Hey, come on, Bidley," he said.

"It's Ridley. And just wait until your father—"

"Well, hi there, young Ridwell!" Howland Burnside boomed as he came down the hall. "I was looking for my boy and I kind of figured I'd find him here since you-all hit it off so well. Now, what was it you wanted from Howly's daddy?"

"I just thought you might like to see—" Lucas began, but Howly cut him off.

"Nothing, Dad," he said quickly. "Bidley and I were just talking, that's all."

"It's Ridley," Lucas said, and smacked the envelope against his palm.

"Yeah, right," Howly said, nodding. "Ridley. I'll remember."

Lucas came back into the room beaming from ear to ear.

"It's okay," he said to Ginger. "He won't tell anyone anything."

"Whew!" Ginger breathed, reaching down to pet Frank.

"Oh, Lucas, those pictures," Arthur said, taking the envelope from him. "Did you look at them?"

"Not yet, why?"

"Well, that's what I was trying to tell you. Most of them came out all right, but there were a few that you must have taken, I believe, that were just black. I guess you forgot to take the lens cap off before you snapped, huh?"

"I know it's early," Arthur said, "but I want to make sure those tickets are there."

"I don't see why we can't stay over one more night," Marcia said tightly. "We'd stay home from work and school tomorrow anyway because we'd get in so late."

"I don't want to take a chance on messing up our flight tickets!" Arthur snapped. "Everyone's flying out of here tonight or tomorrow, and with everything that's happened, I'm sure something would go wrong. And speaking of going wrong, I want to go to the Superdome now!"

"I *don't* want to go to the Superdome now! I'm going to have to spend three hours there as it is!"

Lucas and Ginger sat on the bed and looked from one parent to the other and then at each other.

"I wish they'd quit," Ginger said.

"Yeah, they sound like a couple of—"

"Of what?"

"Kids," Lucas said, and they both giggled.

"All right!" Arthur said, grinding his teeth. "I'll go to the Superdome now with the kids and get the tickets. You and Marvin and Sudie can go sightseeing or whatever and we'll meet later and go to the game!"

"Fine!" Marcia said.

"Fine!" Arthur said.

So there they were, out on the street, getting ready to work their way through the crowd toward the trolley.

"Will we meet Marcia back here afterward?" Ginger asked.

"I guess so," Arthur mumbled.

"Are you sure?" Lucas asked. "I don't remember Mom saying—"

"I'm assuming she'll know to come back here," Arthur said firmly.

"Maybe I better check," Lucas offered.

"All right, check," Arthur grumbled. "Ginger and I will wait in the lobby." He headed back to open the door.

"Oh, listen!" Ginger cried. "There's band music! I bet it's a parade!" She pushed her way toward the curb. "It *is* a parade! Dad, look! Look at the tuba! Lucas!"

But Lucas and Arthur were already inside the Warrington, so Ginger decided to watch by herself. There were two sets of cheerleaders, waving pennants and pompoms, strutting to the beat of the drum.

Then there was another band. Its leaders were carrying a large rectangular banner and Ginger realized the band was probably from a local high school. She couldn't make out the name on the banner so she leaned forward to get a better look and found herself suddenly pushed off the curb. "Hey—" she began, but no one heard her over the noise.

Next, a crowd of fans—some in costume, some with flowers and flags, some in football jerseys and helmets—rushed past, following the bands. Ginger was swept up and carried along with them. She yelled loudly, but everyone was yelling loudly and she couldn't break away without being trampled underfoot.

Lucas and Arthur came out of the hotel together. The parade had disappeared around the corner.

"Where's Ginge?" Arthur asked.

Lucas shrugged.

"There was a parade. I ducked inside before all the people swept by here."

"Did Ginger stay to watch?"

"Yeah, but she was right here." Arthur swiveled his head back and forth.

"Well, she's not here now. I can hear the music. . . . Maybe she followed the band."

"She wouldn't do that. She probably went into one of the stores. Let's give her another minute and wait right here."

"Okay."

After ten minutes, they began to get nervous.

"So," Arthur said, tapping his foot. "Your mom agreed to be back here. What time?"

"Three. Game starts at four, so that gives us lots of time—"

"An *hour*? We still have to pack, Luke!"

"It doesn't take more than ten minutes to pack, Arthur. Don't worry about it. I want to be there on time, too, you know."

"Sure . . . sure, I know."

"Gee, where *is* she?"

"I wish I knew. . . ."

"Look, I'm going to catch up with that band before it's too late and I can't hear the music any more." Lucas turned to go, but Arthur grabbed his arm.

"Come on, Luke, you stay here. I don't want to lose you, too," he said.

"You won't lose me. I know where the motel is. I'll be back here when I find Ginger." He began to run down the street toward the corner.

"Great," Arthur muttered. There was nothing he could do but stand in the middle of the sidewalk and look up and down the street.

When a half hour had gone by, Arthur decided enough was enough. It was time to call the police. He'd just pulled open the Warrington's front door when Ginger came running up, sweaty and panting. Her father took her completely by surprise when he clutched her and hugged her tightly.

"Dad, I can't breathe," she said fuzzily.

He let her go. "We were so scared," he said, shaking his head as if he couldn't believe she was actually there.

"I'm sorry, but it wasn't my fault. I got whooshed off the curb and carried away with the fans. I was hollering my head off, but they thought I was just cheering, like they were. Anyway, I got back here as fast as I could. Where's Lucas?"

"Good question. He took off after *you*."

"He did?"

"Yeah. He was worried."

"He was?"

"He was. Now, look, you wait here. In the lobby this time, not outside. I'm going upstairs to get Marcia before she starts her sightseeing trip."

They were practically hysterical. The desk clerk, the bellmen, the manager, the manager's secretary, even the waiters tried to help, but there was nothing

146

they could do. Marcia stared out the windows of the lobby and chewed on her fingernails. Arthur was right behind her, his hands on her shoulders. Marvin and Sudie sat on the overstuffed couch, Marvin patting Sudie's back while she wrung her hands. Lucas had always been her favorite.

Ginger paced the lobby. She didn't like the way her stomach felt. She didn't care that they were supposed to be upstairs packing and heading out for the game. She didn't care about the *game.*

There were police out looking for Lucas, but as they pointed out, it was like looking for a needle in a haystack. With all those people filling the streets and shops, how could they ever find one small boy?

Suddenly Marcia screamed, "Oh, Arthur! There he is!", and in a split second, she was out the door. Arthur watched her hug Lucas the way he had hugged Ginger.

"Thank God," Arthur whispered as he and the others rushed outside.

"I'm sorry, I'm sorry," Lucas kept repeating. "It was stupid—I found the band, but there were so many people—I kept looking for Ginger, but I suddenly couldn't remember what she was wearing—"

"For Pete's sake, my Bronco's T-shirt," she said.

"Yeah, well—" Lucas stopped to catch his breath. "Anyway, I kept following this parade without looking where I was going, really, and they kept heading into these winding streets."

"Why didn't you stop a policeman?" his mother asked.

"I couldn't find one. Besides, I was sure I could find my way back by myself—" He was cut off by Sudie's massive embrace.

"What time is it?" Ginger asked.

"It's three-thirty," Marvin answered, checking his watch.

"Three-thirty!" Lucas broke away from his aunt. "Let's go! Arthur, come on! Did you get the tickets?"

"With you missing? Sure, the tickets were all I was thinking about."

"We haven't packed," Ginger reminded them.

"We'll stay over," Arthur said. "Somehow we'll fix it with the airlines and the motel." He gave his wife a hug.

"I already fixed it!" Sudie said with a big smile.

Arthur looked at her.

"Well, I just knew you'd change your mind, Arthur," she said.

"Come on," Marcia said quickly, herding her family together. "We've got a Superbowl game to watch! Let's get a cab!"

"I think I hear the kickoff," Lucas said. He was sitting on the sidewalk outside the Superdome.

"Maybe it was just another pregame

thing," Ginger said, hopefully.

"Nah, it was the kickoff."

"Yeah . . . it was."

"Where's Arthur now?"

"Probably murdering Mr. Grapehew or Mr. Hannibal if he can track them down."

"Did he mention all our names at the box office when he asked for the tickets?"

"All of them. Nothing."

"Not even one ticket?"

Ginger put her hands on her hips. "And if they only had one ticket, who would use it, Mr. Brains?"

"My mother," Lucas said, with a wink.

Without meaning to, Ginger laughed.

Arthur and Marcia came out of a side door together. "Come on, kids," Arthur said. He was tight-lipped. There was a large vein throbbing on the side of his neck.

"Where are we going?" Lucas asked.

"Back to the motel."

"What?"

"Shh!" Marcia said quickly. "They

don't have our tickets and we can't get in, so we're going back to the motel."

"But—"

"No buts," Arthur said. "We don't want to miss the game."

"*Huh?*"

"Pass the Fritos," Ginger said, holding out her hand.

"Here. There aren't many left."

"Hog."

"Hey, *I* didn't eat 'em. It was Uncle Marvin."

"Shh!" Arthur said.

They all sat on the beds and floor, the television set in the motel room blaring out the events of the biggest sporting event of the year.

Sudie shook her head. "I can't believe that after all this, you're actually watching the game on TV!"

Arthur glared at her. Marcia did, too.

Frank's ears hurt from the high-pitched noise, so he caught the cuff of

Arthur's pants in his teeth and pulled.

Suddenly, there was a knock at the door.

Everyone looked at each other.

"You expecting someone?" Marvin asked. They all shook their heads.

"Did we order anything from room service?" Ginger looked at her father but then they heard: "Hello, y'all! It's us! The Burnsides!"

Sudie was the one who opened the door and into the crowded room stormed Winnie and Howland, trailed by Howly.

"Thought y'all were goin' to the game!" Howland boomed.

No one said anything.

"Well! Glad you're here. Our reunion's all over and we came right back. It was so late, we just decided to stay over another night. You, too, huh?"

No one said anything.

"Isn't that lucky! Now, we don't care much for football, but we do love people and we think it'd be ever so much fun to just come right in here and watch the game with y'all, wouldn't that be great? Is that popcorn?"

"I don't believe this whole weekend," Arthur whispered to Marcia.

"You sound like you're about to cry," she answered.

"I think I am. Aren't you? Look at this room!"

They looked.

Marvin and Sudie sat on one bed. Sudie was reading a *People Magazine* and doing her nails. Marvin was working a crossword puzzle from the Sunday paper. Howly had decided to sit with them and smear his candy bar on the white bedspread. Winnie and Howland had plopped on the edge of Arthur and Marcia's bed, completely blocking Arthur's view of the television screen.

And Ginger and Lucas sat together on the floor, shoulder to shoulder, quietly discussing the merits of each play.

Marcia gave her husband a hug. "I *am* looking at this room," she said, "and I like what I see."

Arthur smiled weakly. "First we got stuck with Frank, then the plane was delayed, we didn't get our extra room, there was the trouble with the tickets, the Burnsides, not even *seeing* the game after all that—" He rubbed his eyes. "I can't even think of what else happened, can you, hon?"

For a moment, Lucas tore his gaze from the TV set. "Hey, Mom, Arthur," he said. "What a great Superbowl!"